"Do you think you own me, Rafael?"

His fiercely possessive glance answered her. "Yes, I suppose you do," she continued brokenly. "Marrying you was like selling myself to the devil."

"Perhaps our marriage was made in hell," he jeered. "Put our union was legal and binding. You will never be free of my touch or my name!" He pulled her against him, claiming her mouth with a savage sweetness that met bitter denial. A question burned in his eyes as he released her.

"I am in love with another man," Erica said huskily. "I want a divorce, Rafael."

His silence frightened her. Then he laughed, a cold, harsh sound that sent ice through her veins. "There will be no divorce," he said hoarsely.

Let *New York Times* Bestselling Authors

JENNIFER BLAKE

JANET DAILEY

ELIZABETH GAGE

Take you to sultry New Orleans, where passion and scandal are…

Unmasked

MIRA Books
July 1997

Janet

BAILEY

SWEET PROMISE

Harlequin Books

TORONTO • NEW YORK • LONDON
AMSTERDAM • PARIS • SYDNEY • HAMBURG
STOCKHOLM • ATHENS • TOKYO • MILAN
MADRID • WARSAW • BUDAPEST • AUCKLAND

ISBN 0-373-83329-6

Harlequin Presents edition published August 1976
Romance Treasury edition February 1987
Third printing October 1989

Original hardcover edition published in 1976
by Mills & Boon Limited

SWEET PROMISE

This edition published by arrangement with Harlequin Books S.A.

® and TM are trademarks of the publisher. Trademarks indicated with
® are registered in the United States Patent and Trademark Office, the
Canadian Trade Marks Office and in other countries.

Printed in U.S.A.

CHAPTER ONE

THE MUSIC WAS a slow, sentimental ballad, spinning its love theme for the few couples on the floor. The subdued lighting added to the magic of the moment, creating another romantic spell.

A happy sigh slid through Erica's lips as she felt the caressing touch of Forest's chin against her dark hair. Her fingers curled tighter around his neck while she lightly rubbed the side of her head along his chin and jawline in a feline gesture, smiling when she felt his mouth against her hair.

Tilting her head back she gazed into his tanned face, admiring again his striking looks; the commanding strength in repose signified by the square jaw and the cleft in his chin, the sensual line of his mouth, and the velvet touch of his brown eyes as they possessively examined her face.

To speak in a normal voice might break the spell, so Erica whispered softly instead. "Would it sound very corny and silly if I said that I could do this all night?"

"With me or with anyone?" Forest murmured. An eyebrow, the same light brown shade as his hair, arched to tease her.

"That's another thing I like about you. You never take me for granted." Her soft voice trembled with the depth of her emotion and Erica buried her head in his shoulder, knowing her violet eyes were much too expressive of her thoughts.

"What else do you like about me?" His lips were moving against the silken length of her hair again, igniting warm fires in her veins.

"Conceited?" she taunted him, but with a catch in her husky voice.

"Where you are concerned I need all the assurance I can get." The arm around her waist tightened, holding her closer to his muscular body as if he expected her to slip away. "Tell me." His growling order was a mock threat, but one Erica was only too happy to obey.

Hesitant to reveal how deeply she cared for this man who was noted for his careless and carefree association with women, she adopted a light-hearted air.

"For starters, you don't make all those affirmative noises when daddy is around. You're independent and very secure about your own ability. You're much too handsome for a girl's peace of mind. Elusive, always managing to escape being led down to the altar and all the while making a girl believe she's the only one in your life." Erica raised her head from his shoulder and encountered the smoldering light in his eyes. With her lashes, she shielded the answering light in her own eyes. "A girl wants to forget everything her parents taught her when she's with you."

"Not all girls." His hand cupped her chin, lifting it so he could gaze thoughtfully into her face. "Certainly not you. That first night I took you out, I was ready to agree that all those rumors about your being an ice maiden were true. To be perfectly honest, Erica, in the beginning you were a challenge." White teeth flashed as his mouth curved in a rueful smile. "I don't believe anyone has said no to me as many times as you have."

Determinedly she forced herself to breathe evenly. "Do you mean all those times you invited me to your apartment, it wasn't to see your art collection?" she teased, her eyes widening with false surprise.

"Only the one in my bedroom." The laughter left his face as he studied her solemnly. "Every time I touch you or kiss you, I sense that you're holding back. I know you're Vance Wakefield's daughter and many men have taken you out not only because of your looks but because of his wealth and influence. Surely you know me well enough by now to realize that I'm not the least bit interested in who your father is."

"I know that." Their steps had nearly ceased as they absently swayed in tempo with the music.

"Not that I haven't taken into account that you're his daughter to the extent that he is your father and very important in your life," Forest added. "That's the way it should be, even though I know he doesn't totally approve of me."

"It's not you he disapproves of, but your reputation." Erica shrugged weakly.

"And that I may in some way sully yours." He nodded understandingly.

"Daddy isn't an ogre," she said, smiling humorlessly. "He sees me as an adult and realizes that my relationships with other people are on an adult level."

There was no need to add that if Vance Wakefield felt his daughter was being used, he would fall upon the offender with all the weight his power and money could bring to bear. Yet that was not a comforting thought for Erica. In the almost twenty-two years of her life, she had tried very hard to become close to her father. He was a strong, indomitable, ruthless man who despised weakness of any sort. She seriously doubted if he had ever mourned the loss of his wife, her mother, but rather cursed her inability to survive the birth of a child, Erica.

In her early years she had fought for his love, always terrified that her handsome father would marry again and she would have to compete with a new wife and possibly another child for the attention she wanted so desperately. No other woman entered his household, but he became married to his business, a more jealous and demanding rival than Erica could compete against and win. Still she fought and struggled for every ounce of attention that she could steal, using every weapon from open rebellion and stormy scenes to smothering love.

It had taken her nearly twenty years to realize that in his own way he loved her. As strong as the bonds were, she was still a female, hence weak. And Erica concealed any exploit that would point out her vulnerability and lower his esteem of her.

"If it's not your father's wrath you fear, why have you refused me?" A frown of puzzlement drew Forest's brows together. "You aren't an ice maiden—I've discovered that. There have been times when I've held you in my arms that I've been certain I touched a core of passion inside you. Don't you want me as much as I want you? Or don't you trust me?"

"Oh, no, I don't trust myself," she corrected quickly. She could feel the glowing heat of previous shame rising in her cheeks and murmured a silent prayer of thanks for the dimness of the room that concealed it.

"And you've been afraid to do something in the heat of the moment that you would regret in the cold light of day," he finished for her, a gentle and satisfied smile curving the strong line of his mouth.

"Yes, that's what I have been afraid of," Erica admitted. It was a fear that had very firm foundation.

The last note of the song was tapering into silence. For a second, Forest retained his hold, keeping her pressed against his long length, and Erica wondered if he had caught the qualifying statement she had just made. She had been afraid, but she wasn't any longer.

Two months wasn't a very long time in which to know a man. Still, Erica was positive that what she felt toward Forest was not simply physical attraction or even sexual attraction, but a deeper emotion called love, however futile it might be.

A musician in the small combo announced they would be taking a short break and all the couples had left the dance floor by the time Forest guided Erica back to their table. His arm retained a possessive hold on her waist, relinquishing it only when they were seated, their chairs drawn closely together.

"I'm beginning to understand more things about you," Forest said softly, letting his arm curve over the back of her chair to caress her bare shoulders. "But I've been making even stranger discoveries about myself."

"About you? Such as?" prompted Erica, tucking a strand of shoulder-length dark hair behind her ear so it wouldn't interfere with her view of him.

"Such as—" His gaze wandered over her face, lingering on her lips "—I've fallen in love with you, irrevocably and irretrievably in love with you."

Her gasp was a mixture of disbelief and elation. She had never dared hope that he might care as much as she believed she did. The wonder of it darkened her eyes to a royal shade of purple heightened by a diamond mist of happy tears.

"I love you, too," Erica breathed. "I never believed . . . I never thought it was possible that you might love me."

"Only a man in love would take no for an answer as many times as I have." He smiled, and something in his smile confirmed the truth of his words.

She wanted to wind her arms around his neck and feel the warmth of his lips against hers, but just then laughter sounded from one of the tables near theirs and Erica was reminded that they were not alone.

"If you doubted my feelings," Forest murmured, his hand intimately caressing the curve of her neck, "can you imagine how I wondered about yours? I felt you were bound to mistrust me because of my reputation. I've heard some of the stories that have been circulated about me, and some were based on fact."

"It's never mattered to me what others have said about you," she insisted.

She wanted to explain that one of the things that had drawn her to him was his somewhat diehard bachelor attitude, but to do that would mean explaining her reasons and she hadn't the courage for that yet.

"Shall we drink a toast then, to each other?" he suggested. His fingers closed around the stem of his martini glass and Erica reached for her own glass. Compared to his strong drink, hers was an innocuous sherry. Over their glasses their eyes met, sending silent messages while the expensive crystal rang when their glasses touched.

"I think there's something in my martini," Forest declared, drawing the glass near the light after the first tentative sip to study it.

"Besides the olive?" Her tremulous smile was to cover the fluttering of her heart as she covertly studied his profile.

"Would you look at this?" His voice was amused and vaguely triumphant as he directed her gaze to the miniature plastic spear in his hand.

At the end of the spear was the olive with its stuffing of red pimento, but dangling in front of it was a ring. The muted candlelight touched the stone and reflected myriad colors.

"This must be yours." At his announcement, Erica swung her stunned look to him.

"No." Her head moved to deny it.

He had wiped it dry with his linen handkerchief and was now handing the ring to her. "I hope you're going to accept it," he said. "It might be poetic justice to have the first girl I've ever proposed to turn me down. But after all this time of saying no, now that I'm asking you to marry me, please say yes, darling."

Somehow she eluded his move to place the ring on her finger, taking it instead and clutching it between the fingers of both hands. The single diamond solitaire winked back at her, laughing at her until her head throbbed with pain as Erica fought to stem the hysteria that bubbled in her throat.

"Don't you like it?" His voice was low and controlled, but with a razor-sharp edge to it.

The face she turned to him was unnaturally pale and strained. "Oh, Forest, I love it," she gulped, tearing her gaze from the mocking ring to meet his, only to bounce back to the diamond when she was unable to meet the probing brown eyes. A tear slipped from her lashes to blaze a hot trail down her cheek, but she quickly wiped it away. "Please—may we leave here?"

"Of course."

Erica knew Forest would misinterpret her reasons for wanting to go, believing that she wanted a less public place for her tears of happiness. They were tears of happiness. The salty tang of them on her lips was what brought the bitterness and produced the misery of the moment.

With the ease of a man who knew his way about, Forest disposed of their check, produced the light shawl that matched the layered chiffon dress she wore, and had the car brought around to the front of the club.

Moments later he had turned the car onto a quiet San Antonio street and was switching off the engine. Not one word had he directed to her, and he didn't now as he drew her into his arms. Her lips hungrily sought his descending mouth, welcoming and returning the ardency of his touch while his hands arched her toward him. Her unbridled response unnerved both of them and it took some minutes before they were able to recover their powers of speech.

Forest's mouth was moving over her eyes and cheeks. "Will you marry me, darling?" His breath caressed her skin as he spoke. "Or do I have to carry you off into the night until you agree?"

"I want to marry you," Erica whispered, a throbbing ache in her voice. "More than anything else, I want you to believe that."

For all her fervid assurance, his searching kiss stopped, halted by the unspoken qualification in her statement. His tensed stiffness tore at her chest. The ring was still in her hand, burning its imprint in her sensitive palm.

"But I can't accept your ring." She added the words Forest had instinctively braced himself to hear.

"Why?" The demand was combined with the tightening of his hold just before he thrust her away. "You do love me?"

"I love you, darling, honestly I do," vowed Erica, caressing the tanned cheek with her hand. "I simply can't accept your ring. At least not now, I can't."

There was a slightly imperious and bemused tilt of his head. "I've always known you were old-fashioned in some ways, but I never guessed that you would want me to speak to your father first."

"No, that's not what I meant!" Her cry was one of despair and panic.

"I don't understand," Forest said impatiently, wearily rubbing the back of his neck. "Do you want to marry me or not?"

"Yes, I want to—oh, please, Forest, I can't take your ring. It wouldn't be fair." She begged for his understanding, to have the touch of his hands become once more loving.

"Are you engaged to someone else?" An incredulous anger narrowed his gaze.

"No!" She pressed her fingers against the pounding pain between her eyes. "I can't explain and I beg you not to ask me. I swear it's true that I love you, but I need time."

He stared at her for a long moment, his expression carved and impenetrable before a slow smile broke the severe mold. "It is a big step, isn't it? I've had plenty of time to think it over, but I haven't given you much warning."

Time for a decision was not what Erica had meant, but she was very willing to take advantage of it. She opened her clenched hand and stared at the ring. The starlight streaming through the car windows cast a milky sheen on the many facets of the large diamond.

"It is a big step," she agreed, taking a deep breath. "Not something that's done on the spur of the moment." The only smile she could summon was somewhat twisted and wry, its ruefulness concealed by the dimness. "Marry in haste, repent at leisure. I don't want it to be that way with us, Forest."

"Neither do I. I want you to be as certain as I am," he stated.

Although she didn't look up, she could feel the caress of his eyes. The calm determination of his voice almost made her want to put the ring on her finger and damn the consequences, but she steeled herself against doing anything so foolish. Slowly she stretched out her hand to him, palm upward, the engagement ring in the center.

"Would you keep this for me?" she asked. As she met the controlled desire in his gaze, the pain at giving back his ring softened and she sought to reassure him. "I think I'll be wanting it shortly, so please don't give it to some other girl."

"I burned all my telephone numbers weeks ago. There is no other girl." His light brown hair gleamed golden in the pale light as he bent his head to retrieve his ring.

When the ring was safely in his pocket, his velvet brown eyes skittered over her face, its oval perfection framed by the rich brown hair combed away from it. His searching glance came to a full stop on the curve of her lips.

"Don't make me wait too long, Erica." It wasn't a request because of the autocratic ring of his voice. Nor was it a threat, since passion throbbed beneath the surface.

"I won't." The starlight gilded her smooth complexion as she waited in anticipation of the moment when Forest would draw her firmly in his arms.

His hand trailed lightly over the hollow of her cheek back to the base of her neck, sliding under her hair as a thumb gently rubbed the pulsing vein in her neck.

"No woman has ever dangled me on a string before," he told her, his expression paradoxically tender and hard. "I don't like it." Erica started to initiate the movement that would bring her to the muscular chest, but his hand tightened around her neck to check it. Then he released her and turned to the front. "I'm taking you home. I haven't much patience left, so the sooner you make the decision, the better off I will be."

Erica was given no opportunity to argue as he started the car and drove it back onto the street. Part of her wanted the evening to last forever, not to go on torturing Forest as her lack of an answer was doing, but to postpone what she was going to be forced to do if she wanted to marry him. And Erica was certain that she did.

The closer they came to her home on the outskirts of the city, the more her thoughts became preoccupied with her dilemma. When Forest walked her to the door, the kiss she gave him appeared natural enough on the surface, but underneath her nerves were becoming raw from the strain of her decision.

When she stepped inside the house, she discovered her legs were trembling. Their weakness had no basis in Forest's ardent kiss. Her widened eyes, like fully opened African violets, darted to the closed study door, almost the only room in the large, rambling house that her father used. In her mind's eye, Erica could visualize the freezing scorn and contempt that would pierce the blue depths of his eyes if she went to him with her problem.

It had never been his contempt that she had feared. There had been times in the past when she had deliberately provoked his wrath to gain his attention. Only once had her actions backfired on her, the very last time she had done it. Only afterward had she realized how very foolish her childish attempts had been.

But it had succeeded in forcing her to grow up. And Erica had finally realized that her father was incapable of loving her as much as she loved him. In many ways their temperaments were alike. She could be as bullheaded and stubborn as he and just as quick to anger. Yet Vance Wakefield was not able to give of himself and he had never been able to understand her need as a child to be constantly assured of his affection.

Her coming of age had opened her eyes to this one flaw of her father's. In the past almost two years, Erica had stopped demanding more than he could give. Their relationship had reached a peak of casual companionship that she had never thought they could attain. To go to him now would destroy it.

Her teeth sank sharply into her lower lip to bite back the sob of despair. Casting a last furtive glance at the study, she hurried down the hallway to her bedroom. When the oak door was closed behind her, she leaned weakly against it, then pushed herself away to cross the Persian carpet of a richly patterned blue and gold. Her fingers closed tightly around the carved oak bedpost while her darkly clouded eyes stared at the brilliant sea of blue of the bedspread.

Her first impulse was to throw herself on the bed, to wallow in a pool of self-pity that she was ever foolish enough to get into such a situation. Instead Erica shook her head determinedly, banishing the impulse as a waste of energy. She tipped her head back and stared at the ceiling, breathing in deeply to calm her jumping nerves. Low, mocking laughter surged through the tight muscles of her throat, its echo taunting her as it sounded through the room.

"I've spent nearly two years hiding and dreading this day," she chided herself. "I kept stupidly believing that it would all work out on its own."

She buried her head in her hands, refusing to cry as she forced her mind to search for a solution—any solution that would not involve going to her father. Lifting her head out of her hands and letting her fingers close over her throat, she sighed dispiritedly. If only she had someone to talk to, she thought dejectedly. Someone close who would understand what had prompted her to do such a stupid thing. She refused to take the chance of confiding in Forest and risk the loss of his love.

She had no close girl friends, at least, none she would trust with this kind of damaging information. As she was growing up, her father had insisted she attend private schools, snobbishly believing they offered a better and broader education. At the same time Erica had thought he was sending her to these expensive boarding schools because he didn't care about her. Only now could she see that he simply had not known what to do with a young child under his roof. The few friends she had made lived in other parts of the country and after more than four years of separation, correspondence between them had ceased except for annual Christmas cards.

Lawrence Darby, her father's secretary and Man Friday, had always been a sympathetic sounding board in the past, but Erica was totally aware that he automatically carried any major problem to Vance Wakefield, the very thing she wanted to avoid. Not that Lawrence would deliberately betray her; he would only be turning to the man he knew would have the connections and influence to solve her problem.

As for relatives, Erica only had aunts and uncles and cousins, none of whom were overly concerned about her personal problems or even whether she had any. She drew a sharp breath of hope.

"Uncle Jules," she murmured. "Oh, how stupid! Why didn't I think of him before?"

Jules Blackwell was not related to her at all, but he had grown up with Vance Wakefield and was one of her father's rare friends. When Erica was born, Jules Blackwell had appointed himself as her godparent and had taken an active interest in her life. His affection she had never doubted, in fact took for granted. His position and profession were independent of her father's and therefore Jules looked on her father as a man and not the powerful Vance Wakefield. And the man she had affectionately titled "uncle" was aware of the struggle she had made to win her father's love. He could be trusted not to race to her father.

Equally important as all the other reasons was the knowledge that Jules Blackwell was an attorney of some renown. For the first time in nearly two years, the yoke of shame and guilt seemed to ease its ponderous weight from her shoulders and Erica wanted to cry with relief. But the time for weeping was when success was in her grasp.

Dashing to the polished oak chest of drawers, she rummaged through the expensive lingerie until her fingers closed around the knotted handkerchief buried in one corner. Hot color raged over her skin at the touch of the heavy metal object penetrating the material. The red stain didn't leave her cheeks until the knotted handkerchief was buried again, this time in the bottom of her purse.

Sleep eluded her so that most of her rest came in fitful dozes. Still Erica tarried in bed as long as she could the next morning to avoid meeting her father. When she arrived in the sunny yellow breakfast room, only Lawrence was still seated.

"You're late this morning." He smiled, his eyes crinkling behind wire-rimmed glasses. He was only two years older than Forest, yet his receding hairline and thinness added at least ten years.

"I overslept," Erica fibbed, helping herself to toast and marmalade before pouring a cup of coffee for herself.

"Vance has already eaten, but he asked me to pass a message on to you."

"What's that?" Subconsciously she was holding her breath as she took a chair opposite Lawrence.

"The first part was to remind you about the dinner tonight at the Mendelsens' and the second was to suggest that you invite Mr. Granger to accompany you."

Her surprised glance took in the rather smug expression. Her father's suggestions were virtually royal commands, and never before had he even hinted one of her dates should be included in an invitation extended to them.

"Did you have any part in his suggestion, Lawrence?" A knowing smile played with the corners of her mouth.

"No one makes decisions for your father." But there was a twinkle in the pale blue eyes that indicated he had undoubtedly introduced Forest's name into the conversation. "I think Vance is beginning to realize there might be something serious developing between you two."

It was a probing remark designed to inspire confidence, but Erica knew her reply would be passed on to her father. It was his indirect way of remaining involved in her life without taking the time to inquire for himself.

"It's a bit soon to be certain, but it could be serious." It was serious, but Erica didn't want to admit that until she had her other problem solved. "I'll call Forest when I get to the boutique and find out if he's free this evening."

"How is business?" Lawrence inquired.

"I believe Daddy is going to be very surprised when he receives my monthly report," she declared, raising a complacent brow as she sipped her coffee.

More than a year ago Erica had persuaded her father that she needed an outside interest, some reason for getting up in the morning. It was beneath his dignity to allow her to be employed by someone. She was Vance Wakefield's daughter. Erica doubted that her father had actually believed she was serious. To humor her, he had financed the setting up of a small boutique along the landscaped riverwalk.

Along with some of his other traits, Erica had also inherited his business acumen. At the end of her first year in business, the exclusive dress shop had broken even. Now, partly due to nearly flawless taste in fashions and her keen management, it was beginning to show a profit. Being responsible for its success or failure had also made Erica appreciate more the endless demands her father's multiple interests placed upon him.

The instant Lawrence left the breakfast nook, all conscious thought of the boutique vanished. The haste that made Erica leave her toast and coffee half-finished was due to a desire to arrive at the shop and call Jules Blackwell in privacy where there was no risk that her father or Lawrence could accidentally overhear.

The boutique, appropriately called Erica, was already open when Erica arrived. As she locked the doors of her sports car, she said a silent prayer of thanks that she had acquired a clerk as trustworthy and conscientious as Donna Kemper, a petite attractive blonde in her early thirties, divorced and with two little school-age girls. With Donna and a teen-

age girl named Mary who helped part-time after
school, Erica had discovered the shop could survive
without her constant supervision.

There was only one customer in the store when she
walked in. Smiling a hello to the woman, Erica murmured a friendly greeting to Donna.

"The shipment has arrived from Logan's," Donna
informed her.

Erica's head bobbed in wry acknowledgment. "I
have some calls to make, then I'll be out to give you
a hand."

A wide smile of understanding spread across the
fair woman's face. "We've waited this long to receive it. Another few hours before it's on the rack
won't make much difference."

Then the customer required Donna's attention and
Erica walked to the back of the store to the small al-
cove hidden in the storage section. After she dialed
Jules's office number, she sifted through the mail
Donna had placed on the desk, schooling her ham-
mering heart to slow down. It was several minutes
before his secretary was able to connect her with
Jules. He was plainly delighted and surprised that she
had called. The open affection in his voice made her
wish she had done it earlier and not have to seek him
out now when she had a problem.

"I was calling to see if you would be free around
lunchtime, Uncle Jules." Erica explained in answer
to his question.

"Are you asking me out to lunch, young lady?" His teasing laughter lifted her spirits. "Because if you are, I'm accepting."

"Actually, I am," she smiled at the beige-colored receiver, visualizing the rotund, ever smiling face on the opposite end.

"Good. Where would you like me to meet you?"

Erica hesitated. "I...I was hoping I could see you for a few minutes at your office."

Her statement was followed by a small silence before he spoke again, the laughter giving way to solemnness. "Are you and Vance having problems again?"

"No, not exactly," she hedged.

He must have sensed her unwillingness to discuss it over the telephone. "All right. I'll expect you here at eleven-thirty. How's that?"

"Thank you." She sighed.

"Don't worry. Uncle Jules will fix it, whatever it is."

When Erica replaced the receiver, a tentative smile was gleaming in her eyes. With her burden lightened, she telephoned Forest, who very willingly accepted the invitation her father had extended.

CHAPTER TWO

PROMPTLY AT eleven-thirty, Erica entered the spacious reception area of the Blackwell & Todd law firm. The receptionist-secretary glanced up, her keen look appraising the fairly tall, curvaceously slender girl in the simple, elegant dress of vivid blue flowers against a background of white.

"Good morning, Miss Wakefield," she greeted Erica. "Mr. Blackwell said for me to send you right in the minute you arrived."

Erica nodded her thanks, her fingers tightening nervously on the strap of her white purse. Between unpacking the shipment of new fashions that had arrived and waiting on customers, there had been little time to mentally prepare for her meeting with Jules. She would have welcomed a few minutes' delay.

The door to his office was open and a moderately heavyset man was sitting behind the desk, his dark hair liberally peppered with gray as he bent over some papers on his desk. At her light rap, his head raised, the stern expression of concentration replaced by a jovial smile that seemed to better fit his features.

"Hello, Uncle Jules," she smiled, stepping into the room as he pushed himself out of the large leather chair.

"Close the door." His hand wagged in the air in accompaniment of his order. By the time Erica had complied, he was standing in front of her, only an inch or two taller than she was. "I don't want to make my associates jealous when they see me kissing a beautiful young girl," he declared with a broad wink. After he had placed an affectionate kiss on her proffered cheek, his arm circled her shoulders as he drew her toward a large chair near his desk. "It's been two months—no, three months—since I last saw you. That's much too long, Erica."

The mild reproof changed her smile to one of rueful apology. "I'm sorry, Uncle Jules. It doesn't seem that long, but what with one thing or another, time has a way of slipping by."

"From all I've heard, your dress shop is doing well," he said with a nod, forsaking the chair behind his desk for one next to Erica's while he retained possession of one of her hands. "I've also heard you've been seeing a great deal of Forest Granger," he added with a twinkle. "If he's lasted this long, you must be more than just fond of him."

Erica had forgotten how easy it was to confide in Jules. "I am," she admitted, glancing down at the stubby fingers holding her hand. "As a matter of fact, I'm in love with him." She tossed her head back, sending her long brunette hair away from her shoulders and down her back. "Last night, Forest asked me to marry him."

"Mmm." A thoughtfully serious look crept into his otherwise smiling expression. "And Forest Granger has been something of a playboy, loving them and leaving them. Which means his reputation has preceded him in your father's eye. Is that what you wanted to see me about? So I could use my charm to convince Vance that he's the right man for you?"

"No, I...I don't think Daddy is bothered by that." Now that it was time to tell Jules why she was here, Erica found herself faltering. "Daddy isn't going to be a problem."

"But something else is," he prodded gently.

The deep breath she had taken was exhaled slowly so that her affirmative "yes" came out as a sigh. "Do you remember—it will be two years ago this January—when I insisted that Daddy and I take a vacation together?"

"To Acapulco? Yes, I remember," Jules smiled. "As I recall, you came to me then to enlist my persuasion in that effort. Considering the improvement in the relationship between the two of you after you came back, I think spending time alone together was the best thing that could have happened. It's unfortunate that you didn't take a vacation together before."

"The whole thing was a fiasco, a terrible disaster," Erica declared in a trembling voice.

She stared sightless at shelves of law books behind his desk, no longer trying to stop the flood of vivid memories. Her voice was flat and unemotional as she related the events that had taken place. It was a censored version dealing only with facts, but in her mind, Erica relived every moment.

The idea for the vacation had developed from an obsessive need to be the sole object of her father's attention. Only by separating him from his business could she succeed. There were many times in her growing years that Vance Wakefield had hired a female companion and sent Erica off in her company to some exclusive resort. Never once in all her years could she remember her father taking any vacation, any respite from his work.

Enlisting the aid of everyone around her, Erica had forced a reluctant agreement from her father that he should take a vacation. Her first clue that her plans were not going the way she had intended was when her father made reservations for three, ex-

plaining that Lawrence had not had any vacation in
the four years he had worked for him.

Not until they had stepped from the plane and
were registered and shown to the expensive suite of
rooms in one of the luxurious hotels in Acapulco did
Erica fully realize that a vacation to Vance Wakefield meant conducting business long distance. Her
first reaction had been anger, then a complete denial
that she wanted his company at all as she comman-
deered Lawrence with her father's permission.

Lawrence tagged faithfully after her that first afternoon when Erica fled the hotel for the sun-kissed
beaches of Acapulco. Anger tempered with self-pity
seethed just below the surface as she realized that
Lawrence was to be her companion-bodyguard, a
male baby-sitter not much different from the women
chaperones her father had forced on her in the past.
As the toes of her sandals dug into the golden sand,
she knew her father was probably congratulating
himself over his twofold usage of Lawrence: a secretary when he needed him; and a suitable companion to show Erica the sights. And at the same time he
was providing Lawrence with a paid vacation in a
luxury resort. Vance Wakefield was capable of such
a callously insensitive thought.

"Poor Lawrence," she murmured aloud, staring
at the vast expanse of blue water, broken only by

curling whitecaps, the occasional boat and the heads of swimmers.

"Why, poor me?" he asked quietly, stopping beside her, his tan jacket thrown over one shoulder with his tie sticking out of its pocket. The whiteness of his shirt, opened at the throat, accented his pale skin.

"As long and as hard as you've worked for daddy, this is some kind of repayment—being constantly at his beck and call and forced to put up with me," sighed Erica, feeling almost as sorry for him as she did for herself.

"I don't mind." Lawrence shrugged, his light blue eyes gazing back at her through the wire frames.

"Well, you should mind!" The stamping of her feet was negated by the soft sand. "Why should you be responsible for Vance Wakefield's daughter? And I am his daughter, whether he likes it or not!" A diamond mist shimmered over her violet blue eyes as outrage gave way to despair. "Oh, Lawrie, why can't he be like other parents? Is it too much to ask to have him spend two weeks with me? Am I not entitled to two weeks out of twenty years?"

"He isn't like other parents, Erica, because he's Vance Wakefield," Lawrence returned calmly, very accustomed to Erica's swift changes from anger to tears. "You have to see him the way he is, and not the way you want him to be."

"In other words, enjoy the sun and fun of Acapulco but don't make waves," Erica mocked him scathingly. "Forget that I have any rights to his time."

"In his own way, he cares very much about you."

"I'm not giving up." Her voice was low with determination and her chin was tilted at a defiant angle. "Daddy is not going to be able to ignore me for two weeks!"

"Don't do anything foolish," Lawrence cautioned.

Erica didn't answer, but there was a mischievous and challenging glint in her eyes as she hooked an arm around his elbow. "Let's walk down by the water," she commanded.

"We can't go far," he said, leading her toward the gentle waves rolling to the beach. "Your father will be expecting us back."

"So what?" Erica taunted "I've waited for him long enough. Let him wait for me for a change!"

Her rebellious mood brought a worried frown to his thin face, but Erica ignored it. She deliberately focused her attention on her surroundings, absently enjoying the warmth of the sun on her shoulders, glad she had changed out of her heavier travelling suit to the gold sundress with white polka dots. The salty breeze from the Pacific fanned her cheeks, lifting long strands of her hair so it could reach her neck.

Her gaze skipped over the scanty attire of the swimmers and sunbathers, noting instead the thatched, open shelters on the beach to provide places for shaded afternoon siestas. Behind them were the gently swaying palm trees while rows of high-rise hotels formed a necklace for the bay. Beyond them were the mountains, gray, craggy sentinels guarding the golden sand and the sapphire blue sea.

"It reminds me a bit of Hawaii," she commented idly. A laugh bubbled from her throat. "Remember that silly old maid Daddy hired the last time, Lawrie? Prudence Mulier, her name was. She used to get so outraged if anyone tried to flirt with me, but you could tell she was dying for them to look at her."

"Was that the one with the good figure and blond hair that was black at the roots?" he chuckled.

"That's Prudence!" Erica grinned as Lawrence pulled her out of reach of an adventurous wave, its watery fingers stroking the golden sand in front of them. She turned to him eagerly. "Let's wade in the ocean."

"Not me." He shook his head, reaching up to smooth back the hair the breeze had ruffled, revealing his receding hairline. "Go ahead, if you want to."

Before the words were out of his mouth, Erica had
slipped her sandals off and was walking toward the
waterline. The smooth sand beneath her toes was
warmed by the sun, as were the waves that curled
around her ankles. Wading was an ageless sport and
she pitied Lawrence who was too staid and self-
conscious to take part.

Twenty feet or more in front and to the ocean's
side of Erica, a swimmer broke water, rising majes-
tically to stand hip-deep before he began to wade
ashore. The lean yet very muscular torso gleamed
bronze gold in the sun and a medallion winked at
Erica from the cloud of jet black hair covering his
chest. Almost in spite of herself, her gaze raised to
the man's face. Black—his hair, his eyes, his brows,
all were black, glistening and shining from the wetness of the ocean, but no other shade than black.

As that physical impact receded, she was struck by
the aloof arrogance etched in the patrician features,
a ruthlessly molded jaw and chin, high cheekbones,
nobility stamped in the forehead and nose. As Erica
waded closer, their paths intersecting, she was conscious of his height. She was five foot six inches, and
few men towered above her, but this one did.

His glance flicked dismissively over her as he
strode by. Erica was accustomed to a more thorough
appraisal by men. This arrogant rejection stung. She
jerked her gaze to Lawrence, who was strolling out

of reach of the waves, but parallel to her. Her joy in wading in the warm salt water was gone, somehow disrupted by the dark stranger. This dissatisfaction carried her to Lawrence's side, using his arm as a support while she slipped on her sandals.

Yet the pull of the bronze shoulders tapering down to a narrow waist and hips magnetically drew her gaze. There was something very compelling about the man. He was handsome, yet not in the same wholesomely open way of the American men Erica knew. His looks were foreign, ultimately male, striking some primitive chord of attraction inside Erica and creating an impression of underlying steel.

Erica was not aware that Lawrence had noticed the direction of her gaze until he spoke. "He's quite something, isn't he? Lord of all he surveys."

"Yes," she agreed absently, watching the stranger approach one of the thatched shelters nearest them. At the same instant a golden arm reached for a crisply white towel and she saw the woman reclining there.

Even at this distance, Erica could tell that the woman was no longer youthful. Her first instinct was that the woman was a relative until she saw the blond hair beneath the sunhat. There was a flash of white as the man smiled at some comment the woman made. Erica glanced at Lawrence, curious what his opinion was.

"Who do you suppose she is?" asked Erica.

"I don't know what the modern terminology is, but at a guess, I would say he's the woman's lover— for a small fee, of course," Lawrence replied.

"Are you serious?"

"It's a fairly common occupation in resorts like this," he chided her open-mouthed amazement. "A lot of wealthy women come here. I would guess they would be quite anxious to have an escort who looked like that."

Silently Erica agreed, knowing there were some women who would adore that arrogant, lordly air, just as others were drawn to the titles of impoverished counts and dukes. Her back stiffened in anger at the dismissive glance he had given her. She was so anxious to be out of sight of the despicable stranger that she raised no objections when Lawrence directed her back to their hotel.

The following morning Lawrence rented a car. The plans made the evening before were that all three of them, Lawrence, Erica and her father, would take a trip to the colorful open-air market. At breakfast, Vance Wakefield changed the plans, insisting that he had to remain at the hotel because he was expecting an important telephone call.

Resentment smoldered, destroying Lawrence's obvious attempts to lighten the atmosphere and Erica's usual enjoyment of the extensive display of handcrafted items. The only satisfaction she obtained was by flagrantly spending every cent of the money her father had given her. Nearly everything she purchased was designed to anger him.

It was nearly two o'clock in the afternoon when Lawrence drove up to the hotel entrance and patiently unloaded the innumerable packages.

"Do you suppose you can get one of the bellboys to carry all this up to our rooms?" Lawrence asked with a teasing smile, as he wiped the perspiration from his brow. "I'll go and park the car."

Erica nodded reluctantly, feeling suddenly hot, sticky and irritable, and wishing she hadn't given in to such a childish impulse that resulted in the mound of sacks and boxes. Glancing toward the hotel entrance, she searched for the usually ever-present, uniformed bellhops, but oddly there were none in sight. As she pivoted toward the car to send Lawrence to the lobby, it pulled away from the curb. An exasperated sigh hissed through her clenched teeth. It would be foolish for her to leave all these packages unattended while she went in search of assistance.

An impatient movement of her head brought a tall figure into view, lithe strides bringing him closer to Erica. A vengefully haughty expression swept across her face as she recognized the stranger from yesterday. The white tropical suit he was wearing en-

hanced his dark attraction even as he retained that
savagely noble look.

Her hand raised in an imperious gesture to summon his attention. When the glitter of her purple
gaze locked with the blackness of his, it was Erica
who came away with the feeling of being bruised.

"You wish something, *señorita?*" The conde-
scension of his inquiry scraped at her already irritated nerves so that she missed the flawless English
and the seductive pitch of his voice. Her chin raised
a fraction of an inch higher.

"I would like you to carry these packages into the
hotel for me." But it was spoken not as a request, but
as a command. Erica noticed with satisfaction the
hardening of his gaze and the arrogantly arched
brow.

"I do not work for the hotel," he informed her
icily.

The rapier thrust of his gaze sent the adrenaline
pumping through her system, heightening her senses
as she extracted some of her own money from her
purse. The man obviously had an inflated idea of his
own importance.

"That doesn't concern me," retorted Erica, ex-
tending a handful of bills toward him. When he
failed to accept it, her head tilted loftily to one side.
"Aren't you accustomed to accepting money from a
woman?"

Her question was put forth with the unmistakable certainty that the answer was yes. His gaze traveled with insolent slowness over the length of her body until it stopped once again on her face. A mirthless smile curved the hard line of his mouth at the red flags that had run up her cheeks.

A Mexican of shorter stature and a more swarthy complexion appeared at her side, wearing the uniform of the hotel. "Would you like me to take your packages, *señorita?*" he asked in heavily accented English.

Her hand still held the folded bills. Erica looked directly at the taller man. "This man will carry my things," she said to dismiss the hotel employee and thus succeed in putting the stranger in his place, but she wasn't prepared for the torrent of protest.

"Oh, no, *señorita!*" the hotel bellhop declared in a horrified voice. A stream of rapid Spanish followed the outburst while he darted wary looks at the man now regarding Erica with smug amusement.

When the incomprehensible flood stopped, the stranger replied in the same tongue, no doubt guessing by the blank look on Erica's face that she had not understood a word that had been said. Whatever was said seemed to satisfy the bellhop, but the only words Erica was able to distinguish were *turista* and American. She felt their usage had not been complimentary.

Aristocratic fingers took the money from Erica's hand and gave it to the uniformed Mexican. Her mouth opened to make her own protest, but the arrogant stranger forestalled her.

"It is his job, *señorita*." The chiseled mask of his face was inclined graciously toward her. A caustic smile edged his mouth, black lashes veiling the bold mockery of his gaze at the mutinous set of her chin. "Or would you have me take money from the mouths of his hungry family?"

His gaze flicked distastefully over the ill assortment of purchases, arrogantly reminding her that not everyone had an abundance of wealth at her fingertips as she undoubtedly had. And Erica was shamed.

In a sense she had been spoiled since her father had never deprived her of anything money could buy, but she had never flaunted her wealth. And she wasn't about to explain to this stranger the reason for her flagrant extravagance this time, which even she recognized as being childish and in bad taste.

She didn't bother to reply to his taunting question as she pivoted sharply and marched toward the hotel doors with the laden bellhop following in her wake.

ON THE FIFTH DAY in Acapulco, Erica rose early in the morning. Restless and thwarted in her attempts to spend time with her father, she wandered onto the beach, peacefully silent and empty at that hour of the morning. The temperature was mildly warm, although the wind blowing off the ocean was unusually strong. She hoped that an early-morning swim might soothe her restlessness and put her in a better mood before she met her father and Lawrence at the breakfast table.

Slipping off the decorative lace beach jacket, she laid it beside her towel and sandals on the sand. She took her time wading into the warm water, absently watching the soaring gulls. Not until she was almost hip-deep did she realize she had forgotten to put on her bathing cap.

With an irritated sigh, she turned back to the shore. Walking into the waves, she had not noticed the force as they broke around her. Her thoughts had been preoccupied with her father and not on the slight choppiness of the normally calm sea.

Her foot slipped off a seashell at the same moment that a strong wave struck the back of her knees. Already off balance as she was, the wave swept her feet from beneath her, and her cry of surprise was cut off as she was suddenly submerged in salt water. Erica struggled for the surface, trying to get her feet beneath her again. A toe touched bottom. She gulped for air and another wave covered her, its following outward flow dragging her into deeper water.

An iron grip closed over one of her arms, then another hand was taking the opposite shoulder and drawing her to the surface. Instinctively she reached out to cling to her rescuer, coughing out the water she had involuntarily swallowed. Her hands closed around the muscular upper portion of his arms and her legs were weakly supporting her.

"There is another wave coming, *señorita*. Brace yourself against me," a familiar voice ordered succinctly.

In ready compliance, Erica slid her arms around his waist as she reclined her head on his chest. Through the watery spikes of her lashes, she saw the gold medallion in the curling black hairs of his chest.

At that moment the wave broke around them. Its force carried her against him, her motion stopped by the taut muscles in his thighs and legs. The severe constriction of her lungs, robbing her of breath, had no basis in the wave as the water molded her against his body.

When it receded, Erica reluctantly tilted back her head to gaze, rather frightened and bewildered, into his face. A hand left his waist to brush the wet hair from her eyes.

"Th . . . thank you." Her sincere words were met by an impassive look.

"Come." An arm was firmly around her waist and he was half dragging, half carrying her toward shore. "You can catch your breath in shallower water."

Her mind, her senses, her body were in a chaotic state. Her mind was insisting that she reject the gratitude that surged through her toward her rescuer, the stranger who had antagonized her. All the while her senses were reacting to his male virility and her body was still tingling from the burning warmth of his.

They didn't stop in the shallow water but continued all the way to the shore. His arm was no longer supporting her as Erica walked under her own power, his hand firmly resting on her back guiding her steps. When they reached her small pile of belongings, the pressure on her back was taken away, stealing some of the strength in her legs as it went. She sank gratefully to her knees, using the thick towel to rub her shivering skin, wondering how she could be cold when she felt so warm inside.

"It isn't wise to swim alone, *señorita*, especially when the beach is so deserted," he said curtly.

The stern reprimand jerked Erica's head up sharply. He towered above her, his hands resting on the band of his black swimming trunks. Her gaze swung away from the unnerving, masterful stance and searched the empty beach.

"You were," she pointed out crisply.

An eyebrow flicked upward, the small gesture emphasizing Erica's impression that he was not accustomed to being questioned.

"I am familiar with the beach and the tides, *señorita*. You are not."

"No," Erica agreed dryly. "I am a tourist. An American tourist."

The eyebrow descended to its proper place and she sensed a softening in the hard lines of his face. "Who spends many dollars on the handiwork of my country." Amusement glittered behind the mask. "It is good that I saved you to spend more, no?"

"I..." Patches of red appeared in her face at his mention of her embarrassing spree, and Erica bent her head to let the wet hair cover the betraying flush as she reached for her lace jacket. "I'm grateful you were here." But her thanks didn't match the sincerity of her earlier words. "I honestly didn't believe anyone else was around."

"Then it is lucky I saw you as you came down to the beach and heard your cry."

Erica slipped on her jacket and scrambled to her feet, clutching her towel and sandals in front of her as if they were a shield, although her bikini was considerably more modest than some she had seen.

Again she was jolted by the sight of so much bronze skin. Seeing a man in bathing trunks had never disturbed her before. But there was a dangerous fascination to this man, pulling her, compelling her attention even as she reminded herself, in old-fashioned vernacular, that he was a gigolo, escorting wealthy, older women for the monetary favors they would bestow.

"You are not going to swim?" The lilting inflection of his low voice turned the sentence into a question.

Swallowing nervously under the intent regard of his eyes, Erica shook her head firmly. "No. I was only going to take a short swim before breakfast." Her hand self-consciously touched her dripping hair. "My father will be expecting me."

"Of course." He nodded.

"Thank you again," she added over her shoulder as she turned to leave.

"*De nada.*" But there was a vague smile of acceptance on his lips.

Erica wondered a bit breathlessly as she hurried away how devastating a genuine smile of his would be. Then she firmly pushed such conjecture from her mind and fervently hoped she never saw him again.

But she did the following day, although she was certain that he hadn't seen her. He had been with the blonde from the beach. Under the stranger's spell, the older woman had looked quite youthful and animated. Erica had been disgusted.

CHAPTER THREE

ERICA HESITATED on the edge of the hotel grounds. She wasn't in the mood for sunbathing or swimming and she felt if she had to spend one more afternoon staring at the replica of Columbus's ship, the *Niña*, which rested on the beach, she would scream.

They had been in Acapulco a full week. Apart from the marketplace, the hotel, the cliff divers and the beach, Erica had seen nothing. They could have easily been in Miami Beach instead of Mexico for all she had seen of the country.

Her father had even claimed Lawrence, admonishing Erica to enjoy the sunshine. She tucked her book deeper under her arm. It was an interesting and informative book on the history of Mexico that her father had given her. When she had left her father and Lawrence clustered over some figures, she had intended to find a secluded nook in the hotel gardens and read. Now that thought didn't appeal to her.

Sighing dejectedly, Erica turned down one of the garden walks. Her heartbeat quickened as she recognized the figure walking toward her. As yet the dark stranger hadn't seen her. Uncertain exactly why she wanted to avoid meeting him again, attracted and repelled at the same time, Erica tried to dodge behind a high bush and slip through the foliage to another walk that she knew was only a few feet away.

In her haste, she forgot the book tucked beneath her arm and it tumbled to the ground, landing with a resounding thud. For a split second, she froze behind the concealing leaves, staring at the book now lying in the center of the walk. That second's hesitation deprived her of the chance to slip away unseen as the purposeful footsteps slowed as he neared the book.

Silently cursing her ineptitude, Erica stepped into the walkway as he bent over to retrieve her book. "I'm afraid I dropped that," she said stiffly.

"Señorita." He nodded in recognition. There was speculation in the glance that darted from her to the bush.

"I was taking a shortcut to the other path." The defensive thrust of her chin dared him to ask why.

But the glitter of amusement in his dark eyes said he had guessed. His gaze traveled down to the book in his hand before he held it out to her.

"It is a pity to read about Mexico when you are here and can learn about it firsthand," he commented.

His observation was an exact echo of her own sentiments. Her fingers tightened convulsively on the book.

"The way things are going, I'm going to have to be satisfied with this." Anger and self-pity made her voice tremble as it was drawn through clenched teeth. "My father is much too busy for sight-seeing." She darted him a sideways look that didn't quite reach his face, although she was all too aware of the attractive contrast of his white polo shirt and the deep blue trousers tautly molding his thighs. "Thank you for giving me back my book, *señor.*" She started to turn away.

"*Señorita.*" The authoritative ring of his voice halted her, only to become mellow when he spoke again. "I would be pleased to show you around this afternoon if you are free."

"No, thank you." Her denial was vigorous, causing her sable brown hair to dance about her shoulders. Erica didn't care to be exposed to the potent sexual attraction that threatened to captivate her whenever she saw him.

"Why not?" Again there was that impression of arrogance, of a man who was not accustomed to having his invitations refused.

The amethyst pupils of her eyes darkened to plum by her scorn. "I wouldn't like to make your... your lady friend jealous and deprive you of what must be very hard-earned money," Erica stated.

"My lady friend?" His lips thinned as her arrow found its target.

"Yes." Her expression was smugly sarcastic. "The blonde. I've seen you with her several times, on the beach and other places."

"Ah, you mean Helen." He nodded, mocking amusement glittering in his eyes.

"I really wouldn't know what her name is." Erica shrugged. "I simply noticed that the tan she's so keen to acquire only makes her look older."

"I would think someone as young and beautiful as you are could afford to be sympathetic to a woman who finds her beauty fading with each rising of the sun."

The gentle reproof made Erica avert her head. She did feel sorry for the woman, and at the same time contempt that she should attempt to capture her lost youth in this man's arms.

"Perhaps," was the only admission she made.

"Helen is visiting friends this afternoon, so you need not think that you are stealing me away from her by accepting my invitation," he mocked.

"It never occurred to me to try to steal you away." Her eyes widened with genuine innocence.

"Then if you are not burdened by guilt feelings of trespassing and you truly would like to see the city, there is no reason for you to refuse my offer."

His logical statement figuratively removed the ground beneath her feet. "I suppose not," she faltered.

"Then do you accept?" There was a patronizingly inquiring tilt of his head.

"I... I suppose so," she stammered uncertainly, trying to shake off the feeling that she had fallen into some trap he had set for her.

"If we are going to spend the afternoon together, I cannot keep calling you *señorita*." A faint smile edged the corners of his mouth. "What is your name?"

"Erica—" Then she stopped. Even in Acapulco, she had discovered that the name of Wakefield was known. This man already saw her as a rich tourist and she would rather he didn't know how rich. "My name is Erica."

"Erica." His pronunciation lightly rolled the "r", the foreign inflection giving her name a very caressive sound. "My name is Rafael."

Like Erica he added no more than that. Unlike him, she didn't test the sound of it on her lips. The unusual name was too much like its owner, smooth and commanding like satin covering steel, and arrogant.

"Do you wish to notify your father where you are going?" Rafael inquired.

"As long as I am back by five, he won't care where I am," Erica sighed.

Vance Wakefield was too involved in some pending crisis and was too confident of her ability to take care of herself, his trust a compliment if Erica had chosen to look at it that way.

Rafael didn't seem surprised by her remark as he stepped to the side, his hand extended for Erica to precede him in the direction from which he had just come.

"My car is parked over here," he told her.

The car was a very expensive European sports car, its color a highly polished silver gray, the luxurious interior upholstery a blend of black and silver.

"Is this your car or... Helen's?" Erica questioned when Rafael slid into the driver's seat beside her.

The sleek elegance matched the driver, who glanced at her casually before turning the ignition key that sprang the powerful engine to life.

"Do you think I could afford such a model?" answering her question with a question.

"No, I guess not," she agreed with a rueful shake of her head.

The beginning of their drive took them along the familiar bayfront as Rafael identified the small rocky island as La Roqueta, suggesting that Erica take the glass-bottom boat to see the submerged shrine of Our Lady of Guadalupe near the island. When she expressed curiosity about some of the yachts sailing in the harbor, he took her to the docks where many were moored.

He pointed out a mammoth vessel and said, "That is—where I am staying."

Erica glanced at him in surprise. "I thought you stayed at the hotel."

"No, it is only a popular place." Rafael shrugged.

She looked back at the yacht, its name indecipherable at this distance. "Helen must be very rich," she mused.

"I believe she is." He changed gears and turned the car away from the water.

From the yacht club, they went to the San Diego Fort overlooking the bay. Rafael took her through the museum housed in the reconstructed star-shaped fort, the original buildings destroyed by an earthquake. Erica was surprised to discover that Rafael was quite knowledgeable about the history of the area and knew that on her own she wouldn't have found the tour as enjoyable or interesting.

Their next stop was the Plaza de Toros. Erica needed no one to translate the sign. This was the place of the bullfights. She glanced sharply at Rafael.

"I really don't care to go here," she said firmly.

"You don't like bullfights?" The question was asked with the certain knowledge that her answer would be negative.

Erica didn't disappoint him. "No, I don't like bullfights."

"They are only held on Sundays and holidays, and today is neither." A whisper of amusement was in his expression. "I thought you might like to see the inside of a bullring, however empty it might be. Wait here while I get permission to take you in," he instructed.

A few minutes later he returned and guided Erica into the Plaza de Toros, admitted by an elderly Mexican who nodded deferentially to both of them. Erica listened with half an ear while Rafael explained the ritual of the contest, the parts played by the mounted picadors, the banderillos who enabled the matador to observe the fighting characteristics of the bull, and the matador himself who is obligated to execute difficult passes to prove his skill to the crowd.

Mostly Erica was caught up in the eerie atmosphere of the empty stadium, the blood-red color of the wooden barrier that separated the crowd from the ring, the sawdust and sand arena. She had only to close her eyes to hear the cries of the crowd and visualize the black bull charging the magenta cape of a gold-bedecked matador. In spite of herself she shuddered.

"You find the thought of the contest revolting?" Rafael's quiet voice asked.

"I'm afraid I would be rooting for the bull," Erica stated. He was standing beside her, a complacently amused smile on his face. "Have you ever fought a bull?"

"I would guess that all of my countrymen have, if not in reality then in their mind," he replied smoothly, turning his dark gaze on her.

"But you actually did, didn't you?" she guessed correctly. "Why? To prove that man is superior to beast? Or did you simply want to find out how you would react at—what do they call that—the moment of truth?"

"Some consider it a test of manhood," Rafael said sardonically. An enigmatic light in the depths of his eyes held her captive. "But I have found there are much more difficult moments of truth to be faced in a man's life than the one containing a fighting bull. Ones in which a man's future and his happiness hang in the balance."

A spell seemed to be cast on her and it was she who was dangling in the air while Rafael controlled the strings. His words held some portent for her that Erica couldn't understand. Then there was a glimmer of white as he smiled and took her arm.

"Have you seen enough? Shall we go back to the car to continue your tour?"

"Yes, yes, of course," Erica replied, fighting the odd breathlessness that paralyzed her lungs.

The silver car climbed the mountains guarding the city, hugging the switchback curves as it climbed higher and higher. Erica was still inwardly analyzing that moment in the Plaza de Toros while absently responding to Rafael's questions.

Not until they were nearly to the top did she realize that her answers had dealt mainly with her childhood and her relationship with her father. Some defense mechanism in her mind had prevented her from answering in specifics, but thinking back she realized her replies had given him a very accurate picture of her life. She was not normally so open with strangers and she resented his ability to penetrate her reserve.

"And you are twenty years old, you said." His gaze left the road long enough to see her affirmative nod.

"How old are you?" Erica asked quickly.

"Almost twelve years older than you are," Rafael replied, switching down to a lower gear as he braked and eased the car into a wide turnout. "This is what I wanted to show you."

As the car rolled slowly to a stop, Erica stared at the panoramic view before her, barely conscious of the brakes being set and the engine switched off. When Rafael opened her car door, she stepped eagerly onto the gravel.

The vividly blue water of the bay below them was ringed by the golden beach. The multistoried hotels looked more like miniature blocks while the boats on the water resembled grayish white dots. Beyond the city were mountains and beyond the mountains was another range of mountains. The sky was as blue as the sea, its brilliant color only disrupted by thin tails of high filmy clouds.

"At night the view is equally beautiful," he told her.

"I can believe it," Erica breathed, walking forward to expand her nearly limitless view.

"Careful!" His voice rang out sharply at the same instant his fingers closed over her arm, drawing her away from the edge.

The suddenness with which he drew her back made her lose her balance so that she fell heavily against him and his other hand gripped her waist to steady her. Her palms felt the burning warmth of the hard chest beneath his shirt.

"The edge is sometimes undermined," he explained.

Erica's heart was racing, the closeness of his lithe, muscular body erasing any other thought. She tilted her head back to gaze into his face so tantalizingly near her own. His dark eyes were focused on her parted lips, the sensual line of his mouth only inches away.

Erica was consumed by an overwhelming desire for Rafael to kiss her and for a split second she was positive that he would. Then his gaze flicked to the ardent glow in her eyes and he firmly set her apart from him.

She stared at him for a long moment. "Why didn't you kiss me?" she asked, fighting the pangs of rejection.

An expression of amazed amusement lifted one corner of his mouth. "The women of your country are always this forthright, aren't they? They boldly seek out the answers."

The hint of criticism brought a faint tinge of pink to her cheekbones, but Erica wasn't deterred. "If you don't ask, you don't learn," she answered calmly.

"Since you wish to speak candidly, Erica, why did you want to kiss me?" Aloofly he studied her sudden increase of color. "Did you wish to discover if this mystique about Latin lovers was true? A little experiment to brighten your holiday, perhaps?"

Erica averted her head, nervously brushing her hair away from her face. "Frankly, I didn't give your nationality a thought at the time," she answered truthfully.

It was his overpowering maleness that seemed to make her gravitate toward him. She glanced at him from beneath her lashes and saw the faint glitter of doubt.

"It's the truth," she asserted curtly, "although I wouldn't be surprised if your experience puts you in the class of a Don Juan."

"Do you believe the mark of a great lover is the number of women he possesses?" he asked, watching her reaction intently.

"Don't you?" Erica snapped.

"I think the test of a lover is keeping one woman happy for her entire life," Rafael stated, his seductively quiet voice vibrating with firm conviction.

"That—" Shivers raced down her spine at his words. She paused to swallow the sudden catch in her voice before answering boldly. "That still doesn't answer why you didn't kiss me. You said before that I was beautiful."

"A man does not seek outward beauty. That can be found in abundance. It is inner beauty that is rare."

"What about me?" The question was reluctantly asked as she proudly lifted her chin.

"I think," Rafael answered slowly, "that inside you are a bit selfish." He ignored her gasp of anger. "You claim to have deep affection for your father, yet you try to separate him from his work, which gives him great pride and pleasure. If you truly love someone, you want their happiness above yours."

"That's a terrible thing to say!" There was a betraying quiver of her chin. Her hand raised to wipe the vaguely superior expression from his face, but his own lightning quick movement stopped her, her wrist held in a vise grip.

"I was about to add," Rafael continued calmly, a wicked glitter of laughter in his eyes, "that you are very sensitive and would not knowingly hurt anyone."

"Let me go!" Erica tried to twist her wrist free without succeeding. "I don't want you to touch me!"

"A moment ago you wanted me to kiss you." His other hand slipped beneath her hair to cup the back of her head. "Or are you trying to prove you aren't hurt by pretending that you don't care?"

"It's called pride," she said, breathing heavily with anger and frustration. "You should know what that is. You seem to have an overabundance of it."

"I did not kiss you because I don't like being used. And I could not be certain that you regarded me as a man or as a Mexican," he stated.

Erica blinked in disbelief. "How could any woman not be aware of you as a man?" It was a thought she hadn't realized she had spoken until she saw the arrogant satisfaction in his eyes.

There was a fleeting sensation of danger, of being drawn to the edge of a deep abyss and catapulted into its dark depths. The sensual expertise of the mouth that covered hers banished her hold on reality. She should protest, struggle free from his kiss, her mind told her, but with a shuddering sigh she clung to him. Some latent instinct arched her body closer to his, a gesture of surrender.

Immediately his hold on her tightened with crushing suffocation, choking off her breath and strength. And his kiss hardened into possession, ruthlessly staking an ownership that Erica couldn't deny and didn't want to deny.

Then Rafael was firmly untangling the hands she had wound around his neck and placing them at her side. Erica still trembled from her total, elemental awareness of him. The roundness of her eyes gazed into the impersonal mask, her skin tingling with the electric shock of his possession.

"It's growing late," he said tautly, a hand descending firmly on her shoulder and pointing her weakened limbs in the direction of the car. "I will take you back to your hotel."

At that moment his hold over her was so complete that Erica would have jumped off the cliff had he asked. Blinded by the dizzying heights his kiss had taken her to, she found it temporarily impossible to regard him as a paid escort, a fortune hunter, but his distant air when he helped her into the car forced her to do so.

The pangs of humiliation set in as Erica realized the embarrassing position she had placed herself in. She turned her face toward the window to hide the burning surge of heat in her face.

They were halfway down the mountain before Rafael broke the silence. "You should not kiss a man in that way, Erica."

Pride surfaced in a rush of spirit. "Isn't that the way your women usually kiss you?" Keeping her head turned, she made certain she didn't flinch under the obsidian glitter of his swift and thoughtful regard.

"You are not experienced in the fires of passion that can flame between a man and a woman or you would not flirt with them so dangerously," he observed.

"Kissing you doesn't mean I want to go to bed with you," Erica retorted sharply.

"Ah, but when you kiss a man that way, it is he who wants his possession to be complete."

An awkward silence crackled in the air between them as his disturbing statement robbed Erica of any witty reply. Her own response to him was much too vividly recalled and Rafael was not a man to be challenged or bluffed by girlish lies to the contrary.

When he stopped the car in front of the hotel entrance, Erica wanted to dash through the double doors, but she schooled herself to remain in the passenger seat as he walked around the car to open her door. The sun was warm, yet Erica shivered when he politely took her elbow and guided her to the doors. His dark vitality was much too overpowering and his sensual virility made her feel all too vulnerable and young.

Rafael graciously inclined his head toward the doorman who held the gold-enscrolled glass doors. The naturalness of the arrogant superior movement curled her fingers and she stepped a few yards inside the entrance.

"There is no need for you to accompany me any farther," she told him curtly.

His arrogant demeanor didn't change as he turned to her, his head back, his eyes narrowing into black diamond chips. "I hope you found most of the afternoon enjoyable, *señorita.*"

A brow lifted in anger at his sudden reversion to the impersonal term of address. Out of the corner of her eye, Erica saw her father and Lawrence Darby entering the lobby and the sharp questioning look she received when Vance Wakefield saw her with Rafael.

"It was very informative. Thank you." Her nod was condescendingly dismissive.

His gaze centered for a brief moment on her mouth, mocking the coldness that came from the lips that had trembled beneath his.

"*Adios.*" Then Rafael was lithely striding away from her.

Erica hesitated for a second, drawing an audible breath to calm the wild beating of her heart. With a determinedly bright smile, she turned toward her father and Lawrence.

It was unlikely that Lawrence had forgotten that first afternoon when they had seen Rafael with the aging blonde. The polar-blue color of her father's eyes as they met hers told Erica that Lawrence had passed on the information. Refusing to be daunted by his displeasure, she lightly brushed a kiss across her father's cheek.

"If you two will give me a few minutes to change, I'll join you for cocktails before dinner," she said, making her request airy and gay so they wouldn't guess anything was wrong.

"What were you doing with that man?" her father demanded with his usual facility of getting straight to the point.

"Who? Rafael?" Erica inquired with false innocence. "He took me on a tour of the city this afternoon."

"Do you mean you hired him?" Vance Wakefield questioned sharply.

"Yes," she fibbed, adding with an expressive shrug to give credence to her lie, "you and Lawrence were busy this afternoon and I didn't feel like sitting around the hotel."

Vance Wakefield was not an easy man to fool. As he inclined his leonine head toward her, his expression was doubting and laced with penetrating concern.

"You do know what kind of man he is. He's an adventurer, a fortune hunter, living like a parasite off rich women." The undertone of his low voice was warning her in no uncertain terms.

"I know what he is, Daddy," Erica replied calmly.

Lawrence glanced at her apologetically and she smiled in return. To his way of thinking he had only been doing what he thought was best. It would never have occurred to Lawrence to say nothing of their having seen Rafael on the beach.

"That type of man is completely mercenary and without morals," her father continued. "I will not have a daughter of mine getting mixed up with the likes of him. Do you hear me, Erica?"

"Yes, Daddy," she responded patiently.

"I've put up with a lot of your shenanigans in the past, but this is one thing I won't tolerate. Now go and change and we'll meet you in the lounge."

CHAPTER FOUR

VANCE WAKEFIELD never gave warnings lightly and he never saw the need to repeat them. If he ever found out that Erica was attracted to Rafael, however much she fought against it, she would hate to suffer the consequences.

When she had rejoined her father and Lawrence for cocktails, his earlier displeasure must have been placated by her explanation. As if to reward her supposed good sense, he agreed to attend the performance of a locally renowned singer appearing in a nearby lounge the following evening—a concession that surprised Erica since she had tried many times to persuade him to go without success.

The next day, Erica credited her tolerance toward the demands of her father's business to this concession. Her attitude had not been swayed by Rafael's statement that she was selfish; of this she was certain.

The evening of the performance, Erica took special care in choosing what she would wear. Her father had agreed to this evening without any coercion from her and she wanted him to be proud of her. She fingered the cream silk of her long gown and smiled. The silk molded her curvaceous figure, highlighting the darkness of her hair and the violet hue of her eyes.

Picking up her matching evening bag studded with cultured pearls, Erica moved softly toward the connecting door of the suite, rapped once and walked in. Her father was restlessly pacing the room and Lawrence was at the round table, surrounded by papers, with a calculator in front of him.

"You aren't even dressed yet, Daddy?" she scolded lightly.

He halted his pacing, pushed back the cuff of his long-sleeved shirt, then shook his head ruefully. "I didn't realize it was that late," Vance Wakefield replied after glancing at his gold watch.

"Well, it is," Erica smiled good naturedly. "Do you want me to lay out your clothes while you shower?"

"I'm afraid I'm not going to be able to make it tonight, honey," he said as he walked over to take her hands in his.

The absently placating gesture added to the chill that was already shivering over her. For a moment Erica could only stare at him in frozen silence.

"What do you mean?" she demanded hoarsely.

"That Houston deal looks as if it's going to blow up in my face." His sigh accented the lines of strain in his face, but they evoked no sympathy from Erica. "We're going to be lucky if we can salvage it."

"What has that got to do with tonight?" She jerked her hands free. "Houston is more than a thousand miles away."

"I'm expecting some phone calls."

"So? Tell the hotel switchboard where they can locate us or have them take a message!"

"With all the figures and information in the hotel room?" he scoffed. "That wouldn't even be sensible, Erica. We'll simply have to call off tonight, that's all."

"That's all!" Her voice rose shrilly. "I don't know why you bothered to come to Acapulco at all! You haven't even stepped outside this hotel since we came. All you think about is business, business, business! What about me? I'm your daughter! Don't I deserve some of your time?"

"For God's sake, will you listen to reason? This is a million-dollar deal. I didn't just dream up this crisis to avoid taking you somewhere." His own quick temper was beginning to surface.

"Didn't you?" Erica jeered.

"If this silly performance is so important to you," he growled, "I imagine I can spare Lawrence to take you."

"Oh, no." She backed away, her hand rigidly raising in protest. "There isn't any need for you to provide me with an escort. That has always been your solution, but not this time. I'm quite capable of entertaining myself. There isn't any need for you to pay someone to do that. From now on that's going to be my choice!"

"Damn your insolence! You'll be sorry for this," her father declared, trembling with rage.

"I'm not the one who'll be sorry, Daddy. You will be."

And Erica stormed from the room, the telephone ringing just as she slammed the door. Her anger-driven steps didn't slow up until they had carried her through the gardened pool area onto the beach. She paused briefly on the waterpacked sand, then turned away from the ghost ship *Niña* and walked up the beach.

A copper moon floated among the stars, a giant gold balloon in the heavens. Its light gilded the whispering ocean waves with silver, their iridescent sheen adding to the magic of the warm night. Only rarely did the breeze generate enough motion to stir the spiked leaves of the palm trees.

Gradually her steps slowed to a meandering pace. But her frustration still burned inside with a vengeful fire. Her heart cried bitterly at the unfairness of the situation. Erica stared at the gentle waves rolling

onto shore, bringing its treasures to lay on the golden
sand.

A long shadow fell along her side. "I hope you
aren't thinking of taking a swim at this hour of the
night."

Tension thundered through her pulse as Erica
slowly turned to face Rafael, bracing herself against
the force of his compelling attraction. The tip of her
tongue moistened her lips as a fantastic thought entered her mind. She shook the dark mane of her hair
and willed her body to relax.

"Actually I was only admiring the beauty of the
evening," she lied, letting her mouth spread into an
alluring smile.

"It is a tropical night," Rafael observed, not taking his gaze from her moonlit face. "Warm and lan-
guid and tantalizing."

Her heart thumped violently against her ribs. She
felt certain the wild thoughts running through her
mind were visible in her face. What she was contem-
plating was risky, even supposing she could succeed.
Abruptly she turned away from him, momentarily
frightened by what she was going to do.

"Is something wrong?" Rafael immediately
moved nearer as she perhaps subconsciously guessed
he would.

A strange combination of excitement consumed
her as her senses reacted to his vital maleness and her

mind whirled with fantastic revenge. There was light contact of his hand against her shoulder and Erica leaned against it. The warmth of his skin through the tan jacket burned away the last chill of apprehension. Her neck curved sideways so she could gaze into his face.

"Rafael," her voice vibrated huskily. "Will you marry me?"

The dark glow of concern was immediately withdrawn from his gaze and she sensed the freezing aloofness that crept into his shadowed face. Erica turned fully into his now indifferent touch, her eyes roundly innocent and apologetic.

"Have I shocked you?" she whispered.

"The boldness of the women of your country always shocks me. In Mexico, it is the man who is the aggressor." The arrogant flare of his nostrils revealed his displeasure.

Her head was bent in a gesture of contrition. "Yes, I know," she sighed. "It was foolish of me to think you would take my proposal seriously."

Silence throbbed loudly for several seconds before a lean finger touched her chin to raise it.

"Do you truly wish to marry me even though you know—what type of man I am?" Rafael demanded, thick dark lashes further veiling the unreadable expression in his eyes.

Erica blinked back the exultant gleam that leaped into her eyes. "That doesn't matter to me at all," she assured him fervently. Her hand raised in a natural movement to let her fingertips caress his lean cheek. "I only want to marry you, now, tonight."

A muscle in his jaw tightened beneath her intimate touch. "What about your family...and mine?" There was a mocking flash of white teeth at her startled expression. "Didn't you think I had a family?"

"Of course." Her breathing was becoming uneven under his shadowed but intent regard. Erica searched his face in desperation, trying to discern the reason for his reticence. A frightening thought struck her. "Rafael, you aren't planning to marry Helen, are you?"

"Since she is already married, it is unlikely," he answered smoothly. A dark brow arched at her stunned look. "You didn't know that. Perhaps you no longer wish to marry me?"

"No. I mean—no, it doesn't matter," she added hastily, her cheeks taking on a rosy hue. "I want to marry you."

"Tonight? With none of our families present? That is a very selfish request."

"Is it so wrong to be selfish?" Erica whispered, edging closer to him and feeling the touch of his hands on her waist. "Is it so wrong to want this night for ourselves alone? To not want to share this moment with anyone?''

There was a peculiar ring of truth in her voice that even Erica didn't understand. Yet it existed. A marveling light sparkled in her eyes as her heartbeat shamelessly quickened when Rafael's hands tightened about her waist.

Willingly, eagerly, she slid into the hard circle of his arms, burying her head in the hollow of his throat and inhaling the intoxicating scent of his maleness. The firm pressure of his thighs sent scorching fires racing through her blood, leaving her limbs weak and yielding. His low, seductive voice spoke softly in his native tongue, his warm breath stirring her hair.

"Oh, Rafael," Erica moaned. "Please, I don't want to be alone any more."

Again his hand captured her chin, forcing her to look into the unfathomable blackness of his gaze. "Then you must marry me, Erica." Her name rolled caressively from his mouth. "It is I who ask you."

"Yes," she whispered her agreement, wondering at the strange catch in her voice.

There was an ominous sensation that things were not going the way she had planned. She seemed caught in the wake of his dark virility, swept along by forces she couldn't control. Yet this was what she wanted, what she had planned. The risks had all been calculated in that moment when she had formulated the idea. The first obstacle, Rafael's agreement, was behind her. Everything else would occur the way she intended it should. Or so Erica kept telling herself.

WITH A HEART that was light and untroubled, she waited in the foyer of an old but well-furnished building that Rafael had brought her to while he made arrangements for their wedding. This blithe unconcern lasted through much of the ceremony, conducted entirely in Spanish, another reason that made her feel so detached from the proceedings. Rafael's gentle promptings ensured that she made the proper responses to the solemn-faced official.

Then he removed the gold ring from his little finger and slipped it onto her ring finger. Its heaviness, still retaining the warmth of his hand, brought the gravity of her actions to the front. Her gaze tore itself away from the silver eagle with its double head on the face of the ring to look helplessly into his impenetrable eyes. Nervously she moistened her dry lips and swallowed the lump of fear in her throat.

The official's voice had stopped its flow of rhythmic Spanish. Temporarily paralyzed, Erica could only watch as Rafael bent toward her. Her heartbeat fluctuated wildly when his mouth touched hers, breathing warm fires of life into the ice-encrusted regions of her heart. As he drew away, she clung to his arm, nodding in numbed shock at the smiling official and the woman witness at his side.

Distantly she heard Rafael accepting their congratulations while the realization set in that she was married to him. For a moment she was terrified by the swiftness with which it had happened, before she consoled herself that a divorce could be just as quickly achieved. Still her legs trembled beneath her as Rafael led her to the car and her face was paper white. The interior light switched on automatically when he opened the door. His observant gaze immediately noted her pallor, narrowing on it when he slid behind the wheel.

"Are you not well?" His eyes lingered on her trembling lips that still held the sweet taste of his.

Erica ran a quivering hand over her cheek to her hair, half in defense of his regard. "I feel a bit giddy," she admitted, cutting off the hysterical laugh that accompanied her words. "I just realized I haven't eaten since breakfast."

"Then we must remedy that with a wedding dinner, no?" The devastating effect of his smile made her empty stomach churn all the more violently.

"Yes," Erica agreed readily. A full stomach would combat the weakness flowing through her body.

Later she watched as a waiter prepared their steaks on a cooking trolley beside their table. The restaurant had an authentic Mexican air and most of the well-dressed customers were nationals instead of the usual tourists that frequented the hotels. Beautifully scrolled wrought iron separated the dining area from the lounge, allowing the strumming notes of a flamenco guitarist to serenade both sections.

The entire mood of the place allowed Erica to relax and enjoy her meal without any twinge of anxiety. When the dishes were cleared, she picked up her wineglass to finish the last of the sangria. The signet ring on her finger clinked loudly against the crystal, reminding her sharply of her new status. Over the rim of her glass, she glanced at Rafael composedly leaning back against his chair, a thin cheroot between his fingers. Yet there was something very watchful about him. Erica replaced her glass and smiled as naturally as she could.

"Would you excuse me," she asked lightly as she reached for her evening bag, "while I freshen my makeup?"

As she rose to her feet, Rafael was there holding her chair, his gaze flicking over her face as if to decry her need for artifice, but he made no protest. Her pulse beat rapidly in her throat. Erica had to force herself to walk slowly in the direction of the powder room.

By a stroke of luck, a telephone was located near it. In her extremely limited, phrase-book Spanish, she succeeded in having the operator connect her with the hotel. In a nervous, breathless voice, she asked for Vance Wakefield's room.

Triumph glittered in her eyes as she imagined her father's anger when he discovered she had married a fortune hunter. Any thought of his supposedly vital business deal would be vanished at the news. In the blink of an eye he would have the marriage annulled. No doubt there would be a violent scene in which he would vent his wrath on her for doing such a stupid thing, but her father wouldn't be able to ignore her. This time his business would take a second place to Erica!

"Señor Wakefield is not here," the operator's voice informed her.

Icy fingers of panic gripped her throat. "What do you mean, he isn't there? Have him paged," she ordered. "This is his daughter and it's imperative that I reach him."

"One moment, *por favor,*" was the reply.

Her fingers curled tightly over the black receiver as the seconds dragged by. He had to be in the hotel, she told herself.

Another voice came on the telephone, this time a male's. "Señorita Wakefield?"

"Yes, this is she. Where is my father?" she demanded, hysteria edging her voice.

"Señor Wakefield has returned to the States—"

"That's impossible!" Erica broke in. "There isn't a flight back at this hour!"

"I believe he chartered a jet, *señorita*," the man replied patiently. "He has made reservations for you to return tomorrow and has left a message at the desk for you. Would you like me to read it?"

"No," she answered numbly, more to protest the truth of what was being said. "No, that won't be necessary."

"I believe it was an emergency, *señorita*."

"Yes." A bitter laugh stopped in her throat. "A business deal. Thank you. Thank you very much."

Her mouth was twisted in a grimace of irony as she replaced the telephone. His business had won and she had lost. Erica stared at the ring on her finger. She was married and her father wasn't here to rescue her. What was she going to do? What could she do?

Her first instinct was to flee. To get as far away from Rafael as she could, as soon as she could. She could send him a message explaining that it was all a mistake. She hadn't much money in her personal account, but to a man like him, it would be a great deal. But how would she go about getting a divorce? She pressed her hands to her temples, fighting the panic that threatened to surface. She desperately needed time to think. But Rafael was waiting in the dining room for her to rejoin him.

With the same impulsiveness that had got her into this situation, Erica decided to leave a message for Rafael that she was returning to her hotel. The manager could summon a cab for her. In the sanctity of her room, she would come up with a solution. As she turned to carry out her decision Rafael appeared before her.

The color drained from her face at the sight of the compelling figure. Her eyes noted the hard line of his mouth that was momentarily softened by a smile of concern. Cowardice reigned supreme inside her. There was something very indomitable about his personality. Her father might be a match for Rafael, but she wasn't.

"Did you think I wasn't coming back?" she asked with forced gaiety as she glided toward him.

"Should I have thought that?" he returned, thoughtfully watching her swift change from pallor to high color.

"Well," Erica's smile was tremulous as she answered as truthfully as she dared "—I admit to a few jittery nerves like any ordinary bride!"

His regard switched to one of indolence, wicked glimmers of arrogant amusement behind the lazily veiled dark lashes. The firm touch of his fingers on her elbow seemed to enforce his right of possession as he led her into the restaurant proper.

"Those nerves I will allow," he stated. "Do you wish to leave or would you like a drink in the lounge?"

"May we go to the lounge?" Erica requested, stalling for time to cope with this new problem.

The flamenco guitarist was still performing, his agile fingers caressing the strings. The throbbing notes coming from the instrument matched the wild song in her heart. Erica restively held the *marguerita,* a tequila cocktail that Rafael had ordered for her, taking quick sips of the tart liquor, hoping the alcohol would have a calming effect on her jumbled nerves. Her attention was determinedly centered on the musician to avoid the wide shoulders only inches from her own.

"Do you enjoy the music?" Rafael inquired.

"Yes, he's very good." Her gaze bounced away from his face. The aristocratic lines were thrown into sharp relief by the dimness of the room.

"Would you like another drink?"

Erica glanced in surprise at her empty glass and quickly agreed. Time elapsed with unnerving slowness. She consumed the second cocktail and a third, yet she was no nearer a solution than when they had entered the lounge. She didn't dare have another drink since her head was already swimming with the potency of the others. There was no alternative except for her to agree when Rafael suggested they leave.

The freshness of the night air increased the effects of the alcohol. Her nerves were now too relaxed and her mind refused to function properly. Her muteness was traitorous evidence of her cowardice. She sat silently as Rafael started the car and drove away from the restaurant. The bright lights of the hotel row beckoned them, but he was not heading toward them.

"Aren't we going to the hotel?" Erica murmured. A lightning thought occurred to her and she seized upon it immediately. "My things are there. I'll need them."

Once at the hotel, she would be safe. It was suddenly essential that Rafael take her there. In her room she would be able to assert her father's authority. If Rafael should dare to attempt to force his way into her room, she had only to notify management.

"Not yet," Rafael replied, glancing swiftly at the oncoming traffic as he turned down a street. "I thought I would take you to the yacht. Have you ever been aboard one?"

"None of that size," she admitted, her heart sinking as she realized that short of ordering him to take her to the hotel, she had no alternative but to agree. "Isn't Helen there?" she asked hopefully.

"One of the engines is being overhauled, so she is staying with friends," he explained, amusement glittering in the upward curl of his lips at her hesitant question.

"I see," Erica murmured. If Helen had been there, she would have had grounds for refusing to go to the yacht. As it was, she had to resign herself to taking a tour of the ship.

Minutes later they were at the yacht basin and Rafael was switching off the ignition. Erica waited nervously as his tall figure walked around the silver nose of the car to open her door. Again his hand was firmly holding her arm, guiding her along the dock past the silent ships toward the majestic monolith at the far end.

The heel of her satin slipper caught on the ridge of the ship's gangplank, causing her to stumble. Instantly Rafael's arm was around her as he swung her off her feet and carried her the few steps on to the polished deck. It all happened so swiftly that Erica didn't have time to protest, the unexpected contact with his steel-strong frame depriving her of the power of speech. The power of his attraction was never more formidable than at that moment. When he set her on her feet, she leaned weakly against him, her head curved back over his arm.

"Welcome aboard, Señora—" Rafael murmured caressively, his dark head inclining toward her, but his sentence was incomplete as brisk footsteps approached them and he straightened.

"Buenos noches, señor."

Erica blinked rather bewilderedly in the direction of the voice that had granted her a reprieve. A man in a gleaming white uniform stood in front of them, obviously one of the yacht's crew. In spite of the deferential attitude, Erica sensed the curiosity when the man's gaze shifted from Rafael to her.

"Buenos noches, Pedro," Rafael replied. The rest of his swift Spanish Erica couldn't follow, but she thought she guessed accurately that he was explaining who she was and his purpose in bringing her aboard.

Rafael introduced the man as a crew member, Pedro—and the rest of the name escaped Erica in the fluent roll of his Spanish. Unbidden, the thought came to her that she was going to have to learn Spanish since she was married to a Mexican. There was a moment of horror as she realized how permanent she was making the marriage sound. When the man nodded respectfully toward her, she was incapable of speech and her head inclined stiffly in answer.

Sobering instantly, Erica succumbed readily to the pressure of Rafael's hands at her back, eager to complete the tour of the yacht and be taken ashore to her hotel. The change in her manner brought his quizzically watchful gaze to bear on her. She attempted to conceal her haste as he led her into the main salon.

"What is the name of the ship?" she asked, the barest tremor of nerves in her voice.

"She is called *Mañana*—tomorrow." His enigmatic dark gaze held hers. "A suggestion of sweet promise, no?"

There was something suggestive in his statement. Her skin stretched with white tautness over her knuckles as her viselike grip on the pearl evening bag increased. It seemed to her that tomorrow would never come and not with any promise of sweetness.

Turning away from him, she made a show of studying the salon, admiring, in spite of herself, the bold clean lines, the Spanish decor that was elegant and bright. She would never have associated the vivid colors with Rafael's blond mistress. The bold background would not be complementary at all, she decided with some satisfaction.

There was a desire to linger in the tastefully furnished room, but Erica resolutely denied it, and her feet led her into the dining room. She kept her comments to a minimum as Rafael showed her the lounge, the well-equipped galley, and pointed out the direction of the crew's quarters. Her interest was aroused by the booklined study, but she forced herself to glance around with indifference.

"Lastly, the staterooms," Rafael announced.

Erica paused in the carpeted passageway, her gaze sliding away from his lean, aristocratic features. "I don't want to see . . . hers." The admission came out tautly, a strange anger burning in her chest.

"As you wish." Amusement lurked in the mocking edges of his voice.

Rafael opened the doors of two guestrooms for her to see, pointedly ignored a third and fourth door and led her to the last one in the passageway.

"These are my quarters," he told her as he opened the door.

Female curiosity pushed her inside, but the startling decor took her a step farther into the spacious room. The abundant use of rich browns and blacks was arresting, their darkness relieved by a shade of muted gold. There was nothing dreary about it as the atmosphere it generated was luxurious, sensuous and masculine.

Erica pivoted sharply, needing to escape before some mystical spell was weaved. Rafael was standing behind her, his wide shoulders blocking her view of the door. Undercurrents of emotion vibrated the air between them to rivet her feet to the floor. The unwavering gaze pinned to her face, the tapering length of his build, the expensive material of his tan slacks stretched over muscular thighs, the raven blackness of his hair and eyes, the aura of regal arrogance kept her motionless. The air was so charged that Erica hardly dared to breathe.

With slow, deliberate movements, Rafael's hand reached out to touch her cheek, his thumb caressing the bone. His touch released a torrent of desires and her lashes fluttered down to conceal them, steeling herself not to react, not to melt in his arms as she had done before and as Helen had undoubtedly done many times before in the same room. Unexpected pain pressed her lips tightly together.

"No one has been in this room except myself and the crew, Erica."

His uncanny perception of her thoughts opened her lash-shuttered eyes in surprise. The look in his bronzed face Erica couldn't define, but it sent her heart pounding like a trip-hammer. His thumb moved down to the corner of her mouth and traced the outline of its feminine softness. When his hand moved to the side of her neck, her lips trembled in unwilling protest to its departure.

The descent of his dark head was unhurried, her lips parting in anticipation of the moment when Rafael would claim them. His kiss was a lick of flame, igniting her already kindled desire. Possession was immediate with no tender, probing search for a response by Rafael.

A swirling mist of lascivious weakness swayed Erica against him. Her shoulders were seized as she was pulled to the rock wall of his chest. The mastery of his embrace was a seduction of the senses. The total exploration by his mouth of her face and neck and shoulder was beyond her power to halt had she wanted it to stop. He alternately gave and took, demanded, received and returned her ardency.

In a moment, she would be lost beyond recall, absorbed by a personality more forceful than any with which she had come in contact. It was this fear that enabled her to whirl away from him when every other warning had been swept aside.

Her freedom of his touch was only for an instant as her hair was brushed aside and his mouth sent tongues of wildfire along the sensitive cord of her neck. Erica gulped for life-giving air, her trembling fingers closing over the lean hands spreading across her stomach, drawing her back against his rising male hardness. One hand allowed itself to be pushed away. Her success was met by failure when Erica felt the nearly silent sound of the zipper sliding open down her back. She ached to feel his touch against the nakedness of her flesh. The intoxicating desire to submit was overpowering.

She turned back toward him, her hands clutching the bodice of the cream silk gown that threatened to slip away. Her face reddened as she saw his gaze lingering on the tantalizing shadow between her breasts. Mutely she beseeched him with her luminous eyes.

"Do not be ashamed." His seductively soft voice caressed her. "You are my wife, Erica." Again the smoldering light in his eyes swept over her breasts, the intimacy of the look causing her to draw a deep breath that only made the light burn brighter when it returned to her face. "Every inch of you is beautiful to me. Don't be frightened, *querida*."

Strangely Erica wasn't frightened. Her arms willingly wound themselves around his neck as he carried her to the bed, setting her on her feet beside it. She was his wife, he had said. A delicious sensation of bliss washed over her. It was right that he had such power over her.

His jacket was off, his shirt unbuttoned and being tugged free of his trousers. The sight of the golden tan chest, the naked skin being revealed as he removed the shirt, brought the last vestige of resistance. Her fingers tightened convulsively on her loosened gown.

"I...I have to go back to the hotel...now," she said huskily.

Rafael looked at her for a long moment, his arms gently circling her. "If that is what you wish, *querida*, I will take you there," he murmured. "Speak now or let us speak no more."

But the fruit of temptation was there before her and the age-old desire to bite into its sweetness was supreme. Her hands slipped around his waist as she tilted her head to receive his kiss.

Later Rafael kissed the blood from her lips inflicted by her teeth when she attempted to bite back her cry of pain. He cradled her in his arms, murmuring reassuring words in Spanish that she didn't understand. Tenderly, patiently, he waited for the agony to subside before he initiated her to the dizzying rapture a man and woman can attain. When the last sigh of ecstasy shuddered through her, he possessively held her against his own chest, pressing her head to the uneven beat of his own heart.

"Esta mañana, querida," he whispered softly.

CHAPTER FIVE

ERICA STIRRED restlessly beneath the leaden band that held her down. The pressure eased slightly and she shifted into a more comfortable position on her side. In a state of near-wakefulness, she became conscious of an alien warmth against her breast. Instantly all her senses were alert, her skin tingling where the hand possessively cupped the rounded firmness of her breast. Then the rest of her body became aware of Rafael lying beside her.

Gently she rolled away from his unresisting hand, hugging the edge of the bed in case she had awakened him. Her mind raced in panic as she stared at the shadow-darkened form in the bed. What had she done? Horror and shame ate at her insides. How could she have been so permissive as to go to bed with this man, this virtual stranger, simply because some Mexican official had mumbled a few legal words that she hadn't understood?

This man who had erased her innocence forever was an adventurer, a fortune hunter! How could she have allowed herself to be seduced by him? Her fa-

ther would have forgiven her for marrying him if he
had arrived in time. But now, once he learned how
weak she had been, Vance Wakefield would never
forgive her.

Erica backed away from the bed in terror. Franti-
cally she grabbed at her gown lying on the floor and
the rest of her garments scattered nearby. Keeping an
eye on the still figure in the bed, she dressed with
fear-driven swiftness. Her muscles were stiff and re-
sisting. Guilt turned her stomach with sickening
movements at the cause for the soreness.

Carrying her shoes and evening bag in her hand,
she tiptoed into the hallway, quietly closing the door
of the stateroom behind her and listening for any sign
that Rafael might have heard her leave. The only
sound in the entire yacht was the waves licking the
sides of the structure. Pausing in the doorway to the
deck, Erica glanced furtively around, afraid of running into one of the members of the crew. Nothing.
She hurried as quickly as she dared to the gangplank
and didn't stop running until she was ashore.

The sky was pitch black. By the time she was able
to wave down a cab and arrive at her hotel, the first
glimmers of dawn were lighting the sky in the east.
The night life of Acapulco ran from dusk to dawn,
so there were few glances from the hotel staff at her
early morning return.

Once in her room, Erica walked directly to the shower, discarding her gown in the wastebasket and willing the sharp spray of water to banish the licentious memories that burned so vividly. It was futile. They were seared there beyond recall.

As she reentered her room, the door to the connecting suite opened. For a split second, she froze in terror, half expecting to see Rafael standing in the doorway. Instead it was Lawrence, a maroon robe tied around his waist, his fingers raking his thinning hair.

"I thought I heard someone stirring in here." A yawn punctuated his sentence. "What are you doing up at this hour?"

Erica was between Lawrence and the bed. Chances were he hadn't seen that it hadn't been slept in and he obviously believed she had come in much earlier. She was too ashamed and humiliated by her own conduct to tell him what had happened.

"I'm getting ready to leave," she replied tautly.

"Vance had a maid pack most of your things." A sleepy smile crooked the corners of his thin mouth. "He left me behind to see that you made the plane—which, by the way, doesn't leave for hours."

Something told Erica that if she didn't leave the hotel within the hour, Rafael would be here to get her and the whole sordid story would be out.

"We're leaving now," she declared.

Lawrence frowned. "There aren't any scheduled flights at this hour of the morning."

"Then we'll charter a plane like Daddy did!" A strange mixture of torture and temper stormed in her eyes. "But we're leaving now!"

There was a wry shake of his head as if he gave up trying to understand what caused her mercurial moods. "I'll meet you downstairs in twenty minutes."

Only after Lawrence had left the room did Erica notice she was still wearing Rafael's ring on her finger. She hurriedly stuffed it in the bottom of one of her suitcases and got dressed. Three-quarters of an hour later, their chartered plane was leaving the runway with not a sign of Rafael anywhere.

They didn't return to San Antonio but flew to Houston where Vance Wakefield had gone. He was too involved in negotiations to notice Erica's agitated behavior. The rare moments he spent in her company were too short for her to confide in him had she gathered the courage. It was nearly three weeks later that they returned to their home in San Antonio.

"SO I NEVER TOLD DADDY," Erica sighed as she finished telling her story to Jules Blackwell. "I've never told anyone until today."

"And you say the marriage was consummated?"

"Yes," she nodded, not trying to hide the scarlet shame in her face.

"Now, now," he said, patting her hand affectionately. "Don't start chastising yourself again. It seems to me that you've punished yourself enough."

Erica smiled at him ruefully. "Thank you for not telling me how foolish I was for getting myself into this mess."

"Hindsight isn't going to get you out of it." His round figure was pulled out of the chair beside her as he walked around to his desk. "You haven't seen this fellow since you left Acapulco, have you?"

"No, I haven't."

But she remembered those first months of fear when she had waited out those long days not knowing if she was pregnant and wondering which day Rafael would appear, to blackmail her. And there had been the anxiety that her unprincipled response to his advances meant she was promiscuous. Her subsequent severely controlled behavior with other men had since earned her the nickname of ice maiden that Forest had teased her about.

"Do you know where this man lives? Is his home in Acapulco?" Jules asked.

"I don't know." Erica shook her head.

"What is his full name?"

She looked into his gently inquiring gaze, a bubble of hysterical laughter escaping her throat before she could stop it. "I don't know. San Antonio has always been my home, but I grew up in boarding schools. I never learned basic Spanish other than good morning and thank you until last year. I took private lessons so I could converse with some of the customers in my boutique. But then—" she shrugged "—in Acapulco, I couldn't follow the pronunciation. Isn't it funny, Uncle Jules? I'm married and I don't even know what my name is."

"What about the marriage certificate?" he asked, not giving her a chance to dwell on another example of her stupidity.

"Rafael must have it. I vaguely recall signing my name. I suppose he put it in his pocket."

"It's a legal document, so it will be on file. I can get a copy of it," he assured her as he removed the ring from the handkerchief Erica had given him. The silver eagle with two heads stamped on the face of the ring stared back at him. "This signet ring could be a family crest, but it's unlikely."

Erica watched the attorney anxiously. "How much do you think I'll have to pay Rafael for the divorce?"

"It depends on how wealthy he thinks you are and whether he has discovered you're Vance Wakefield's daughter," Jules answered. The look he gave her was sincerely apologetic. "I'm sorry, Erica, but your husband—"

"Don't call him that!" her tempestuous pride made her snap.

He smiled understandingly, silently glad to see her stoical regret had not completely replaced her spirit. "Very well, this man is obviously mercenary. I doubt if he'll settle for a small sum."

"I don't have a great deal of money, Uncle Jules, outside of the allowance Daddy gives me. You know how the trust fund is tied up." Her teeth nibbled at her lower lip. "Daddy will ask all sorts of questions if I have to ask him for a large amount. He would probe until he found out why I wanted it. We get along so well now." The last sentence was a despairing sigh.

"I know."

A mirthless smile lifted the corners of her mouth. "If I'd had an affair with Rafael, Daddy could have forgiven that. But to marry him! And keep it a secret all this time. I simply can't let him find out no matter how much money Rafael demands. I'll have to find a way of raising it on my own."

"You're worrying about a bridge we haven't reached, my dear," Jules scolded. "There's time enough for that later when I've located this man." He held out his hand to her. "Are you going to take me to lunch or not?"

His gruff tone was meant to cajole her out of her worry. Erica laughed easily and reached out to take his hand. "Of course!"

After lunch, they paused outside the river walk restaurant. Jules's jovial expression was converted to professional reassurance.

"I'll make a few discreet inquiries when I get back to the office," he promised. "I'll let you know as soon as I find out anything."

"It would be better if you contacted me at the boutique. I don't want Daddy getting suspicious," Erica returned. She hesitated for a second. "When you do find Rafael, I . . . I don't want to see him."

His wink said he would take care of that. "Give Vance my regards."

"I will, Uncle Jules, and thank you."

He waved aside her thanks as they parted. Following the meandering San Antonio River to her shop, Erica discovered she wasn't as relieved as she had thought she would be. Her burden had been lightened and she was confident that Jules Blackwell would be able to find Rafael and arrange the divorce. Yet she was restless, curiously on edge, as if there was something she hadn't taken into account.

The ominous gray cloud was still hovering on the horizon when she dressed for dinner that night. The vibrantly yellow cocktail dress she wore was chosen especially to chase it away. Erica tried to derive satisfaction at the calm way her father included Forest in the conversation en route to the Mendelsens' home. Vance Wakefield could be quite cutting if he didn't like or approve of a particular person. But her inner preoccupation made her gaiety forced, although no one appeared to notice except herself.

John Mendelsen greeted the trio at the door of his Spanish-style home. He was a distinguished-looking man, a contemporary of Vance Wakefield's and a sometimes business associate, friend and golfing partner. His pale blond hair had long ago lightened to silver and the leather tan of his skin contrasted sharply with it and the ice blue of his eyes.

"Where's that dark-eyed wife of yours?" Vance demanded in a laughing voice.

"Luisa is on the patio with the rest of our guests. You're the last to arrive, as usual, Vance, but there is still plenty of time for a couple of drinks before dinner," John assured him. "I'm certain Luisa will stop flitting among our distinguished guests long enough to see that your thirst is satisfied."

"Luisa is much too aristocratic to flit," her father corrected.

Erica smiled a silent agreement. John Mendelsen's wife was a petite but imposing woman, a member of an old and respected Mexican-American family, innately proud and regal.

"Who has your philanthropic wife invited this time?" Vance asked as John began leading them through the cool hallways. "Should I have brushed up on my Spanish?"

"We have our usual group—George and Mary Saunders, the Cliftons, the Mateos and their daughter, and Reina Cruz." Their host shrugged. "If Luisa seems to be preening a bit, it's because she succeeded in persuading Torres to come this evening. He's the head of an old Mexican family and an authority on Latin-American history. He's in San Antonio to oversee a new exhibit at the Mexican Cultural Institute. Have no fear, though. He speaks perfect English." Erica and Forest were walking a few steps behind her father and John Mendelsen. With the two older men deep in conversation, Forest leaned slightly toward Erica.

"Have I told you how stunning you look?" he murmured in a low, growling undertone as his eyes ravaged her face.

She darted him a sparkling, flirtatious smile. "No, tell me."

His hand tightened around her waist. "If we were alone, I'd do more than tell you."

Erica glanced up to his face, noting the ardent light in his warm brown eyes. Only for a second her imagination played tricks on her and she saw smoldering black eyes. Her stomach constricted painfully before she could blink away the tantalizing image and she was once more seeing the square jaw and dimpled chin belonging to Forest.

"Have you mentioned us yet to your father?" Forest asked.

"I haven't said yes to you yet," she whispered with forced lightness. In her heart, she knew she couldn't give him an answer until the arrangements had been made for her divorce from Rafael.

"But you will say yes. If I wasn't positive of that, I..." They had arrived at the patio and Forest was unable to complete his sentence.

Erica understood the urgency in his voice. In a lesser way she felt the same. Since that long-ago night with Rafael, she had learned that she was neither permissive nor promiscuous. Her laxity that night had been caused by a combination of circumstances.

The first of the guests to notice their arrival on the patio and to step forward to greet them was Reina Cruz, an attractive vivacious widow in her late thirties. Her smile encompassed all of them, but Erica thought it lingered a little longer on her father. In the past if any woman had singled her father out for attention, she would have disliked her on the spot. But her recently acquired, mature attitude toward her father no longer dictated such a reaction. She liked and admired Reina and even wished her good luck should the woman choose to pursue her father.

"I have heard a great deal about you, Forest." Reina smiled after Erica had introduced him. "I am glad to meet you. Erica is very lucky."

"I hope to make her luckier some time soon," Forest replied, flicking a possessive glance to the dark-haired girl at his side.

"So you've arrived, Vance." Their hostess moved gracefully to the quartet.

"You know I wouldn't miss one of your dinner parties, Luisa," her father declared in his typically diplomatic and offhand way.

"Erica, you look lovely." The still-dark-haired woman brushed her cheek with a kiss that was composedly affectionate without being overly so. Just as graciously, she turned to Forest. "And I'm so glad you were able to come, Forest."

"It was thoughtful of you to invite me," he nodded.

Luisa's dark eyes sparkled at Erica. "It seemed the best way to ensure that Erica could join us."

She felt her father's eyes rest on her thoughtfully, but Erica made no reply to the leading comment except to smile calmly. Luisa Mendelsen linked her arm with Vance's.

"Come, all of you. I want you to meet my guest of honor," she said.

Luisa was very active in civic organizations and projects dealing with the Spanish-American heritage of Texas and San Antonio in particular. Her dinner parties usually included a Latin-American dignitary, cultural, political, or artistic, so Erica was not surprised that one was here this evening. She glanced idly ahead of her father and their hostess to see the elderly historian from Mexico.

Among the familiar faces of the other guests was the foreign visitor—tall, bronzed, hair and eyes of pitch black. Erica's knees almost buckled beneath her. Her vision blurred and for a second she thought she was going to faint. Briefly she leaned against Forest before her sight cleared and blood flowed again to her limbs.

Controlled by a numb sense of inevitability, Erica let Forest escort her to Rafael, bracing herself for the moment when he would see her. As if from a great distance, she heard Luisa's voice call to him and the dark, arrogant face that she knew so well turned in answer. The aloof gaze swept the group. Erica couldn't be certain, but it seemed as if his gaze narrowed for a lightning second on her before it stopped on Luisa. A polite smile lifted the firm line of his mouth, firmer than Erica remembered.

"I would like you all to meet Don Rafael Alejandro de la Torres," introduced Luisa.

Erica dug her fingernails into the palm of her hand. She glanced anxiously at her father as he was presented to Rafael. There was no recognition in his face. Any second she expected Rafael to blurt out that he was Vance's son-in-law, then gradually she realized he wasn't going to.

"This is Vance's daughter, Erica Wakefield."

Luisa's voice directed Rafael's gaze to her. The lean, chiseled mask was molded by courteous lines while the rapier thrust of his gaze stripped what little color remained in Erica's face. There was a jeering arch in one black brow.

"You are not married, Miss Wakefield?" Rafael asked dryly as he offered his hand in greeting.

Her hand trembled as she forced it to touch his, remembering the way those lean fingers had caressed her body with erotic intimacy. That same heat seemed to scorch every inch of her.

"No, I'm not married," she denied. Her quivering chin lifted proudly.

Then her hand was released and Rafael was turning toward Forest as Luisa made the introduction again, adding an explanation that he was Erica's friend. There was no reaction by Rafael to that statement. A servant arrived with a tray of drinks. Instantly the other guests, friends of long standing, moved forward to greet them and Erica was able to slip away from the circle that included Rafael.

Yet the abandon with which she threw herself into the conversation with the new group didn't make Erica any less conscious of Rafael's presence. Never once did she look in his direction, but she saw the way the other women's eyes gravitated toward him. At times, she could hear his low-timbred voice, and icy chills of apprehension danced along her spine.

Had he come here to find her? Was the exhibit at the Mexican Cultural Institute just a pose? Or was he an imposter? In Acapulco he had admitted to being a fortune hunter. Erica herself had seen him with a woman many years his senior. He had remained silent about their marriage. Did that mean he intended to blackmail her? There was no question any more that he knew who her father was.

Erica knew she had to find out where he was staying so she could let her Uncle Jules know. Yet she shrank from inquiring directly, and asking the others at the party would only arouse curiosity. Forest, what would he think? Her head pounded with the multitude of her questions. She hadn't wanted to see or speak to Rafael again, but the choice had been taken out of her hands.

If Rafael's plans were to blackmail her, then to run, to avoid seeing him would show cowardice and increase his hold over her. Perhaps the best thing would be to seek him out, apart from the others, and let him realize that she wasn't afraid of him. But it was inconceivable that such an occasion would arise. His being, his personality were too compelling for him to be alone in a group of people unless he chose it. A despairing cloud darkened her eyes to a royal shade.

Dinner was announced. Erica discovered her father was seated opposite Rafael, who was on the hostess's right, while she was down the table and across from him, a position that promised that any time his gaze looked down the table it would include her. Even Forest was separated from her so that she could no longer use him as a shield.

The carefully prepared meal was tasteless. Erica spent most of her time pushing the food around her plate and making sure her eyes didn't stray to Rafael. Tension was beginning to etch tight lines around her smile when the dessert dishes were cleared and Luisa suggested they move to the living room.

Forest started toward her, only to be waylaid by George Saunders. Rafael was talking to her father a few steps away and Erica glanced desperately around for a haven. With a smile of relief, she saw Julie Mateo, only a year younger than herself, just entering the living room.

"What have you been doing lately, Julie?" Erica asked brightly to draw the girl to her side.

"Very little, actually. Helping out at the hospital part-time." She was a quiet, unassuming girl with auburn hair and pleasing features. It had only been in the past few months that Erica had got to know her very well. "I like your dress. Is it from your shop?"

"As a matter of fact, it is," Erica admitted with a self-consciously proud smile.

"That's an excellent way to advertise your boutique." Julie grinned.

"Do you own a boutique, Miss Wakefield?" There was a knowing gleam in Rafael's eyes as he watched the startled turn of Erica's head.

"It's a joint venture between my father and myself." In spite of her efforts to reply calmly, her voice sounded cool.

Vance Wakefield smiled at her indulgently. "I have to admit my daughter has a sound business head. She picked out the location on the river walk and except for a little advice from me, she has operated it all by herself."

The raven-black head tilted patronizingly toward her. "Your shop on the river walk, is it called Erica's?"

"Yes, yes it is," she answered defensively. "Not very original, I admit."

"What a coincidence!" One corner of his mouth moved in a mocking smile. "I stopped there today, close to noon, to buy a gift for my sister. I'm quite sure I would have remembered if I had seen you there, Miss Wakefield.''

''I believe I was out to lunch at that time,'' she said, her expression freezing as the irony of the situation struck her. The very hour she had been discussing her elopement with him to Jules Blackwell, Rafael had been in the boutique. ''I hope Donna was able to find a gift suitable for your sister.''

''She did.'' The instant the reply had been made, Rafael turned to her father, a suggestion of boredom in his features both with Erica and the subject of the conversation.

''What do you think of San Antonio, Don Rafael?'' her father inquired. ''Have you been here before?''

''Not for some time,'' he replied, answering the last question first. ''San Antonio is like an aging dowager, really proud of her rich heritage and culture, and futuristic in her outlook. Yet she has never lost the grace and old-world charm she was born to possess. She truly deserves to be one of the four unique cities in the United States.''

Erica stared at him in silence, stunned by the way he had put her feelings toward the city into words. She had forgotten how very charming Rafael could be. How she hated him at that moment! It took all her willpower to prevent her from telling the entire gathering what a despicable person he was. He had married her for her money and he was here to collect some of it.

Her rage seethed like a cancer inside her as she watched the way his presence dominated the room. The center of interest was always where Rafael was. Erica stood on the fringes of satellite groups, not trusting herself to speak for fear she would be pronouncing her own death sentence as well as Rafael's. And the subjects of the other guests' discussions never seemed to stray far away from Rafael.

When the small group she was standing with began to gravitate toward him, Erica pretended an interest in a statue of Aztec origin. Forest was on the far side of the room leading some discussion with Matt Clifton and Ed Mateo. Both were nodding agreement to what he was saying. She tried to be glad that Forest was mingling so well with her peers, but she wanted to be gone from this house and Rafael, to feel the comfort of Forest's arms around her. From past experience, she knew the party would drag on for another hour or more.

"The statue is an excellent example of early Aztec art." Erica's back stiffened as her head jerked sideways to see Rafael standing negligently by her side. His black gaze ridiculed the impotency of the anger in her expression. "I'm afraid this will have to do," he murmured mysteriously.

A confused look entered her eyes as she regarded him haughtily. "I don't know what you mean."

"I believe you wished to speak to me privately. This is as private as we can get, unless you wish to cause comment by leaving the room in my company," he mocked.

"What are you doing here?" Erica hissed, staring at the statue and wishing she could throw it at him.

"Didn't our hosts explain? I am here with an exhibit from Mexico," he answered in an amused voice.

"Don't play games!" she snapped, whirling about to face him. "You know very well what I'm talking about!"

Her anger seemed to amuse him more. "Do you truly wish to discuss it here, *mia esposa?*" Erica caught her breath sharply as his eyes seemed to physically touch the upper portion of her body, travelling with unnerving slowness. "You are my wife, Erica de la Torres, by word and by deed."

Coloring furiously at his unnecessary reminder, she glared her resentment. "No, we won't discuss it here," she admitted grudgingly.

His superior nod of acknowledgement indicated that he had known very well that it could be no other way. "I am staying at Palacio del Rio," and he gave her his room number. "May I expect you there at noon tomorrow?"

"Yes," she snapped.

"I shall look forward to the pleasure of your company," he said as the sensual line of his mouth curved tauntingly.

The only satisfaction Erica could acknowledge was the fact that Jules Blackwell and not she would meet Rafael tomorrow. At least, she would be spared another disturbing encounter with him.

As Erica predicted earlier, all the guests lingered for better than an hour. Rafael was standing with Luisa and John Mendelsen as the others bade them goodbye. Forest was standing behind her, his arm loosely circling her waist so she rested lightly against him. There was a sense of protection in his casual embrace as they waited for her father to finish speaking to his host.

"I didn't truly expect to enjoy myself tonight," Forest murmured near her ear. "Your father's friends aren't nearly as stuffy as I expected them to be."

Erica bent her head back and to the side to gaze into his ruggedly handsome face. "I would have much rather been somewhere else," she said decisively.

"Damn, but you're beautiful!" Fire leaped into his brown eyes as his lips possessively touched hers, unmindful of watching eyes.

Erica held his ardent gaze a second longer, his tender caress touching her deeply, before she turned to see if her father was ready to leave. Her softly luminous eyes were pinned by the ominous blackness of Rafael's, his nostrils flaring in arrogant disapproval. Erica's heart catapulted in fear at the ruthless lines etched in the handsome, bronze mask. Then he turned away and she was free, but she wondered how long it would be before she was truly free.

Later, in her own home, Vance Wakefield discreetly made himself scarce so Erica and Forest could say their good-nights in private. Erica went eagerly into his arms, responding with forced ardor to his kisses. Yet she found she couldn't block out the events that had taken place.

Worse, she discovered herself trying to compare her reaction to Forest with the way she had felt with Rafael. Even when she had disliked Rafael in Acapulco, she had admitted that she was sexually attracted to him. But a comparison was foolish. Sensations aroused by the first time that a man awakened a woman to her inner physical desires would never be as stunning or overwhelming again.

CHAPTER SIX

ERICA PRESSED a hand to her churning stomach, then pulled open the door to the hotel's riverwalk entrance. She had telephoned Jules the instant she had arrived at the boutique that morning. The receptionist had informed her that he was out of the city and not expected back until Tuesday or Wednesday of the following week.

A half a dozen times during the morning, Erica had walked to the telephone to cancel her appointment with Rafael. As reluctant as she was to see him again, she was also aware that she desperately needed to know what his demands were so that she would have time to raise the money. The sooner she found out how difficult a task it was going to be, the sooner she could find a way of accomplishing it. Besides, she wasn't certain she could put Rafael off until Jules came back. It was conceivable that he might try to contact her at the boutique or at home.

There was no sign of Rafael in the restaurant on the river level and none in the lobby's cocktail lounge. Her watch showed exactly twelve noon. With her heart beating unevenly, Erica walked to the house phone and dialed his suite. Her hand nervously clutched the white receiver.

"Yes?" His rich voice flowed smoothly in her ear.

"Th-this is Erica." She faltered momentarily. "Shall I meet you in the lounge?"

A mirthless chuckle sounded on the other end of the receiver. "You indicated that you wanted a private discussion, then you pick a public gathering place to have it. Do you not wish to speak to me where no one can overhear?"

"Yes—"

"Then come to my suite," Rafael commanded, and the line was disconnected.

Erica held the phone to her ear for a long moment, her throat choked by the words of refusal she hadn't had the opportunity to say. Mutely she rebelled against the conspiracy that continued to give Rafael control.

Replacing the receiver, she walked self-consciously toward the elevators, glancing furtively around her in case someone she knew saw her. It was one thing to pretend that she had accidentally bumped into Rafael in the crowded lobby and it was another to be seen going into or coming out of his room.

Luck was, for once, on her side as the doors yawned to admit her to an empty elevator. There was no one around on Rafael's floor, either, and Erica walked swiftly to his room, praying that he wouldn't make her wait too long in the hallway before opening the door.

When it opened, she quickly darted in, not drawing a secure breath until she heard the door close behind her. Then she swung to face Rafael. The upheaval going on within caused her considerable consternation as she tried not to notice how effectively the azure blue suit complemented his dark coloring and increased his attraction. His hand made a politely mocking gesture toward the burnt-orange cushions of a small settee. Erica walked stiltedly toward it, trying to calm her chaotic thoughts and emotions.

"Sherry?" Rafael offered a stemmed glass of the amber liquid to her.

She accepted it, more to have something to occupy her hands to ease their nervous trembling. The last thing she wanted was drink to cloud her thinking. This was the moment that she needed all her faculties alert.

Hitching his trousers, he sat down in a bulky-styled Mediterranean chair next to the settee. His manner reminded Erica of a lord dutifully about to listen to the problems of one of his lowly subjects. Indignantly her lips tightened.

"You wished to discuss our marriage," Rafael prompted with infuriating calm.

"I wish to discuss our divorce," she corrected him curtly.

"Why have you waited a year and a half to make your wishes known that you want our marriage to end?" His voice sounded disinterested, but his unreadable dark eyes had grown blacker.

Erica glanced down to her glass. "I didn't know how to reach you or where you lived."

"And you made no effort to find out," he stated.

"No." She refused to be intimidated as she lashed back sarcastically, "I was simply glad to get away from a fortune hunter like you!"

"Ah—" a mockingly complacent smile widened his mouth "—but you learned last night that my profession was not what you imagined it to be."

"If you are who you say you are," she answered coldly, then shrugged. "Either way, it's immaterial. I want a divorce."

"Last night I heard talk that you and this Forest Granger are in love." The soft jeer sliced out at Erica. "Perhaps he is the reason for your sudden decision."

Her chin raised to a defiant angle. "We are in love with each other. Now, will you give me a divorce?"

Rafael lifted his sherry glass to the light. "I am Rafael Alejandro de la Torres." A black brow arched derisively toward her. "I realize the name means nothing to you, but in my country, it is synonymous with pride, honor and influence. I am the eldest male of my immediate family, thus the one in command. The traditions and religious beliefs of my family will not permit a divorce—on any grounds.''

Ice ran through her blood, sending shivers of terror to every extremity. Erica stared at him blankly, refusing to believe that she had heard what he said. Somehow it was imperative for him to realize her position.

"I don't think you understand." Her voice was small and weak. "I don't love you. I'm in love with Forest!''

The shining dark head inclined arrogantly toward her. "Are you asking my permission to take him as a lover?''

"No!" Her protest was unmistakably shocked and indignant.

"That is good, because I would not permit you to disgrace my family's name.''

"You would not permit me!" Erica's cry was one of outrage. "No one dictates to me! I do as I please!''

"You are Erica de la Torres and you do as *I* please,'' Rafael informed her tersely.

Her anger was nearly beyond control as she rose on shaking legs, her hands doubled into fists at her side. Rigidly she stared down at him, fighting to check her temper.

"I am not one of your meekly submissive countrymen. I will not be at the beck and call of a domineering male, ever!" she declared tightly.

A cold anger spread over the lean features. He
pushed himself out of the chair to tower in front of
her. "Have I ever given you any reason to believe
that I would mistreat you?" he demanded.

"No." Erica faltered slightly under his menacing
gaze. "But it wouldn't frighten me into cowering in
front of you if you did. I will not allow you to try to
dominate me!"

His expression immediately altered into one of
mocking amusement. "If a person is domineering,
querida, he uses physical force to have his wishes
carried out. Domination uses superior intelligence
and knowledge. It would be wise to differentiate between the two in the future."

"Don't twist words," she protested, spinning away
from him. Anger evaporated as hopelessness drained
its source. In a last gambit to persuade him to change
his unyielding stand, she turned over her last card.
"I'll pay you anything you ask."

"Money will not buy me a legitimate son of my
blood," Rafael stated.

"A son?" gasped Erica, whirling around to search
his aloof, arrogant face.

"Does the thought of bearing my child offend you?" His head was thrown proudly back as he intently watched her reaction.

His child, a miniature version of the man before her. Erica's mind reeled at the thought, yet not with distaste. She shook her head to chase away the image.

"I find it offensive to be your wife," she said instead.

His hand touched her shoulder. Impulses of disturbing awareness tingled down her neck. She pivoted sharply away from his hand.

"You did not always find my touch repulsive," Rafael murmured, his eyes narrowing at her apprehensive expression.

"I was young and inexperienced, but you changed all that," Erica retorted.

"You are my wife. That hasn't changed."

"Then change it! Divorce me!" she demanded vigorously.

"I have already explained that it is impossible," he stated.

"If you don't willingly grant me a divorce, I shall sue for it," she threatened. "I will not be married to a man I don't love!"

Rafael's lean jaw was tightly clenched, a muscle in the side rebelling against the iron control. The fury in his darkened eyes reminded Erica too late that he was of Spanish descent. The blood of cruelty ran in his veins. The fine suit he wore was merely a cloak of civilization to conceal the primitive savagery she had noted before.

"That is something you should have considered before you married me," he snapped harshly.

"I did consider it." The fear that nearly paralyzed the workings of her lungs was masked by a show of bravado. "I never intended the marriage to last more than an hour. The only reason I married you was to get back at my father for always putting his business ahead of me. I knew he would have our marriage annulled that same evening."

"But your plan backfired, no?" Rafael smiled.

Erica turned away from that complacently arrogant expression. "Yes, he had flown back to the States—on *business*," she admitted bitterly.

"Why did you not tell me of this that night?" he asked with ominous quiet.

"I was afraid of you then," she tossed over her shoulder. "I was no match for you. I thought if I could go back to the hotel I would be safe. Only you didn't take me back to the hotel."

Rafael studied her thoughtfully. "Was it cowardice that dictated your submission to me?"

Erica swallowed nervously. The memory of his fiery caresses brought a disturbing ache to the lower areas of her stomach. Tongues of shame licked her cheeks as she remembered the way she had welcomed his intimate touch.

"Of course," she breathed. "That's why I ran at the first opportunity." It took all of her pride to look into his face without faltering. "How can you possibly want to remain married to me when you know why I did it? When you know I love someone else?"

"What I want and what I must accept are two very different things, Erica," Rafael stated grimly.

"I won't accept it!" Her cry rang angrily through the room. "I'll have my attorney start the divorce proceedings immediately."

"I shall fight you, Erica," he told her coldly. "The newspapers will sell many copies with the names of Wakefield and Torres emblazoned on the front page. And you do not want that kind of divorce. You want a quiet one so that your father will never find out what you have done. It would be interesting to discover what your boyfriend's reaction would be when you are involved in the scandal I would create."

"You wouldn't," Erica whispered. Her rounded eyes searched his ruthlessly set face for some indication of compassion.

"I would."

Trembling fingers touched her pale cheeks as she took two shaky steps away from him. She believed that he would do everything he said.

"I can't just simply announce that I'm married to you," she murmured.

"I will be in San Antonio for several weeks—with the exhibition. We will go through the motions of a courtship. People have fallen in love in less than a few weeks. Another wedding ceremony can be arranged for the benefit of your father and you can return with me when I leave for Mexico," Rafael stated.

"But I'm not in love with you," Erica repeated again. "I love Forest."

"In time you will forget him," he declared arrogantly. "This is not the type of marriage I would prefer, either, but we must deal with reality. Perhaps one day we both may derive some measure of satisfaction from it."

"No," she protested weakly. He was asking her to commit herself to a life sentence with him. Blackmailing her not for money, but for her life, her happiness.

"There is no alternative, Erica. If you are so foolish as to fight me in this, I will go to your father and tell him of our marriage. I do not think he will understand your motives for marrying me nor your actions on our wedding night. A messy divorce would not be to his liking, I think."

Erica knew her father too well not to admit that much of what Rafael said was true. Yet surely there must be another way. She hugged her arms about her to ward off the cold chill of inevitability.

"I can hear your mind racing," Rafael mocked. "I don't ask you to agree with me today. I will give you a week to think over what I have said. You will see that to become my wife is the only amiable solution."

"I must have sold my soul to the devil when I married you," Erica murmured hoarsely. "Or else I married the devil."

"Perhaps it is a marriage made in hell." His derisive jeer disturbed the bronze mask. "But it is no less legal and binding. That is what you must remember."

His words echoed in her mind all the way back to the boutique. Erica had escaped from him once, but it had never really been an escape, merely a postponement. If she ran this time, Rafael would unhesitatingly go to her father and they would both hunt her down. Her anger had not moved him. Her appeals for his understanding, his pity, or his mercy had not touched him. Rafael wanted her as his wife to keep his family tradition unblemished and to bear him a child. He did not care that she didn't love him. Her wishes or desires mattered not at all to him.

As she pushed open the shop door, Erica knew she would never be able to get through the afternoon pretending that nothing was wrong. The throbbing pain in her temples was nearly blinding her. Her statement to Donna that she wasn't feeling well was barely out of her mouth before her assistant was agreeing with her.

"Go on home, Erica. I didn't think you were feeling well this morning. Now there's hardly any color at all in your face. I'll take care of everything."

For the rest of the afternoon and all of Sunday, Erica shut herself in her room, using the pretense of illness to break her date with Forest. Each passing hour made her realize there were only two choices, as Rafael had said. And she rebelled against both of them.

She alternately pounded her pillow in anger and sobbed into it from frustration. Restlessly she paced the floor like a frightened and disoriented caged animal. Her only choice was which of the two evils would she choose. Did her father's love and respect matter more to her than her own future? A messy divorce might even lose her Forest's love and hence her future. His career was only now bringing him fame and success. The publicity and notoriety that Rafael promised would accompany any divorce action she started could destroy Forest's career should he stay involved with her. How long would Forest love her when he saw every one of his ambitions dashed to the ground because of her?

Yet Erica couldn't conceive of actually becoming Rafael's wife. Undoubtedly he was handsome and obviously the head of a very respectable family. But she had always wanted her husband to cherish and adore her, to give her all the affection that her father had not been able to demonstrate. Was she fated to spend the rest of her life never feeling loved? Rafael did not love her. He wanted a wife. It wouldn't have made any difference if he had loved her. She still loved someone else.

Monday morning arrived and she was no closer to a decision. But Erica knew she couldn't keep hiding in her room. Besides, Rafael had given her a week to make up her mind. Perhaps a miracle would happen. Maybe her uncle Jules would have a suggestion to make when he returned. With that slightly encouraging thought, Erica allowed herself to become absorbed in the work at the boutique.

Forest had a meeting to attend on Monday evening, so it wasn't until Tuesday noon that she saw him. He took her to lunch at one of the sidewalk cafés on the riverwalk. They sat in the shade of an umbrella, a tenderly possessive light in his eyes whenever he looked at her.

Erica toyed with the guacamole salad she had ordered. "Are you very ambitious, Forest?" she asked lightly.

"Of course I am," he replied. His gaze was speculating as it touched her downcast face. "There was something behind that question, wasn't there?"

She tried to shrug it off, wishing she hadn't tried to find out what his reaction would be. But Forest didn't accept her easy dismissal of the subject.

"Honey, are you afraid I'm marrying you because I think your father can further my career?" he asked softly, a teasing note of reproof in his voice.

"No," Erica assured him quickly, gazing into the ruggedly attractive square-jawed face. "I know how very much it means to you that you've achieved the success you have because of your own ability."

"Then why the question?" An amused frown creased his brow.

"I was...only wondering how important your work was to you," she hedged.

"A man's work is his life." There was still a puzzled gleam in his velvet brown eyes. "I know how much you resented the demands your father's empire made on him. You aren't asking me to give up my career, are you?"

"Would you if I did?" Erica tried to make it sound like a joke, as if his answer didn't matter.

"No," Forest stated unequivocally. "I love you very much, but you'll have to marry me the way I am."

"Oh, darling, I do love you the way you are," she whispered, sorry she had ever made him doubt it.

The dimple on his chin deepened as he smiled. "Then you'd better hurry up and say yes so I can put that ring on your finger."

A noncommittal statement sprang to her mouth, but it never got beyond her parted lips. An ashen pallor stole over her face as she saw Rafael approaching their table in the company of another man.

"What a pleasant surprise to see the two of you again!" he greeted them when Forest glanced away from Erica's face.

"Don Rafael," Forest acknowledged, rising to his feet.

Rafael's eyes were mockingly amused when he saw Erica hide her shaking hands beneath the table.

"I'd like you to meet Señor Esteban Rivera, a noted archaeologist of my country," he said, introducing the man standing beside him. His identification of Erica and Forest to Señor Rivera was done in Spanish.

"Buenos dias, señorita, señor." The man nodded graciously to them both.

"It's a pleasure, Señor Rivera," Forest said, smiling.

Accustomed now to conversing with Mexican-American customers in her shop, Erica automatically replied in the man's native language, adding that she hoped he was enjoying the beauties of San Antonio. She thought nothing of it until she encountered the piercing intentness of Rafael's gaze.

In deliberately rapid Spanish, he demanded, "How long have you been fluent in my language?"

Erica glanced hesitantly at Forest, whose grasp of Spanish was very limited. He was quite plainly curious at what was said and a little suspicious of the tone.

"I have only recently learned Spanish," she answered Rafael in English, her tone stiff and defiant. "It is useful in my shop."

"Of course." Rafael nodded.

"Would you care to join us for coffee?" Forest offered.

"I'm sorry. Señor Rivera and I have another engagement. Perhaps another time," he replied, deferring the invitation with a patronizing tilt of his black head.

"Why do you suppose he stopped?" Forest mused thoughtfully after the two men had disappeared.

Erica shifted uncomfortably. "I imagine he was just being polite."

"Maybe." But Forest wasn't convinced and neither was Erica.

Jules Blackwell called her at the boutique the following morning, before she had an opportunity to see if he had returned from his trip.

"I have made some discoveries, Erica. Some of them may surprise you," he told her, continuing before she had a chance to tell him of Rafael's presence in San Antonio. "Your husband is not a fortune hunter. Far from it. My dear girl, you married into a very old Mexican family that has holdings in Central and South America."

"I know. Uncle Jules, he's here—in San Antonio," she said.

There was a moment of startled silence. "Have you talked to him?"

Erica sighed heavily and proceeded to tell Jules of what had transpired while he was gone. When she concluded, it was he who sighed.

"This puts an entirely different complexion on things, doesn't it?" Erica could visualize the frown of concentration. "I guess I could go to see him at his hotel. At this point, it certainly can't do any harm."

"Would you, Uncle Jules?" Emotion choked her throat.

"We can't give up without a fight, can we?" he asked, back to his usual jovial voice. "I'll call you right after I see him."

Then he hung up.

"YOU'RE AWFULLY quiet tonight, Erica," Forest commented, trailing his fingertip over the pensive line around her mouth. "Is something troubling you?"

"I was thinking." Erica breathed in deeply and glanced about the intimate lounge.

"About me, I hope." He smiled and his arm tightened affectionately around her shoulder.

"Actually about the shop," she laughed. In truth, it had been about her conversation with Jules Blackwell. He had called back the following afternoon after having met Rafael. He had been unable to persuade Rafael to revise his stand. When she had asked his advice, Jules had hesitated, then insisted that this was a decision only she could make. He refused to advise her one way or the other.

"Having problems at the boutique?" Forest asked.

"Nothing important." Erica shrugged.

"Then let's talk about us instead of the shop," he murmured.

"N-not yet." She swallowed nervously, knowing there was no way she could tell him that there might never be an "us."

He sighed impatiently and moved away from her, darting her an angry glance that couldn't be mistaken even in the dim light of the room.

"I'm sorry, Forest," Erica apologized. "I don't have an answer for you and it isn't fair to lead you on. I'm trying to be honest with you." As honest as she could in the circumstances.

"Thanks." Caustic bitterness ate into the edges of the word. He stared at his drink for an uncomfortable moment. Then his gaze slid to her face. "You didn't deserve that. It's my turn to apologize, honey."

"I understand," she said, nodding.

"Well, well, well. Will you look at who just walked in?" he murmured cynically. "I wonder if it's another coincidence."

Erica glanced toward the entrance and immediately averted her head when she recognized the tall dark figure just entering the lounge. Her heart skittered wildly along her ribs. Nervously she clutched her glass, wishing she could make herself small so that Rafael wouldn't see her.

"Is he coming here?" she asked tautly.

"He's with some other people," Forest replied, watching with undisguised speculation. "They're taking a table on the other side. I don't think he's even seen us. I guess I was wrong."

A nervous laugh of relief bubbled from her throat. "What ever made you think Don Rafael was following us in the first place?" she chided.

"I don't know." He shrugged, glancing at Erica, then back to the table where Rafael was seated. "I had a hazy impression at the dinner party the other night that he was interested in you. He always seemed to know where you were and who was with you."

Her cheeks flushed hotly. "You must have been mistaken. I didn't notice that he paid any special attention to me," she protested with false lightness.

"It was just an impression. I didn't say it was right." He smiled a crooked smile. "Tell me, did you notice him?"

"Oh, Forest!" Erica tilted her head to one side in simulated amusement while her mouth felt unnaturally parched. "He's an imposing man. A woman would have to be blind not to notice him, and even then she would probably pick up his vibrations."

"Do you know, I've never been jealous before?" He chuckled. "Dance with me, Erica. I have this terrible need to hold you in my arms."

His arms held sweet torment. She felt that she had to savor every moment they were together in case it was their last. She might never again be able to know this sense of security and well-being. The song ended much too soon, forcing her to open her eyes and move away from Forest's broad chest.

Her gaze focused immediately on Rafael sitting at a table on the edge of the dance floor. Sardonic amusement etched the blackness of his eyes as they shifted their glance to Forest. It was impossible for her not to acknowledge his presence without being blatantly rude. She tried to force polite words of greeting from her trembling mouth, but Forest was already filling the void.

"We meet again, Don Rafael," he said politely.

Rafael rose and extended a hand to Forest in greeting, leaving him with no choice except to cross the few feet to accept it. Introductions were quickly made of the two couples accompanying Rafael before he insisted that Forest and Erica allow him to buy them a drink.

Erica silently raged at the way Rafael was maneuvering events. She had wanted this evening with Forest to be special. She wished she could have had the courage to persuade Forest to leave when Rafael had arrived at the club, but she hadn't wanted to arouse his curiosity. Now she was seated between Rafael and Forest, feeling stiff and uncomfortable, knowing that Rafael had arranged it this way deliberately.

Her skin went hot as Forest rested his arm along the back of her chair as if staking his proprietorial rights to her. Her violet eyes darkened with resentment that she couldn't respond as she wanted to Forest's touch. Rafael's presence was an all-too-potent reminder that she wasn't free. As if feeling her censure, Rafael glanced at her, a mocking awareness of her thoughts in his eyes.

The conversation had been following an impersonal line until Forest suddenly asked, "I don't believe you have mentioned whether you were married or not, Don Rafael?"

The color drained with sickening rapidity from Erica's face. One corner of Rafael's mouth lifted in a humorless smile as he pointedly stared at her.

"The woman I have chosen has not yet consented to be my wife," he stated ambiguously, letting his indolent gaze slide back to Forest's tightened jaw. "But I have no doubt that she will soon make her decision."

Forest glanced quickly at Erica, a suspicious jealousy darkening his usually soft brown eyes. Her hands were rigidly clasped in her lap, as she tried to ignore the crackling electricity in the air.

"Perhaps, Don Rafael," she murmured in an even voice, "she needs more time." Deliberately she looked at Forest. "Marriage requires the commitment of the rest of a girl's life."

"I agree, Miss Wakefield," his seductive voice mocked her. "To leap into it hastily could have disastrous results. A life of repentance would not be pleasant for either party."

One of the other members of his group spoke up and the subject was gratefully changed. Erica knew that she had sidetracked Forest's suspicions by looking at him when she had made her comment to Rafael, but she despised herself for tricking him that way, just as she despised Rafael for putting her in the position where she was forced to do it. She wondered what form of retribution he would extract, then his next words to Forest left her in no doubt.

"Do I have your permission to claim this dance with Miss Wakefield?" he asked.

To refuse would make Forest appear churlish. In the next instant, Erica found herself accepting Rafael's guiding hand as he led her onto the dance floor.

When he turned her into his arms, Erica wondered how she could have forgotten how very powerful his physical attraction was. Her senses vibrated with the provocative nearness of his thighs and the spread of his lean fingers on her back. She hated this awareness of a man she didn't love.

"Why can't you leave me alone?" she whispered tautly, staring at the whiteness of his shirt collar and idly wondering if he still wore the gold medallion.

"I thought women liked to have their husbands pay attention to them," Rafael mocked.

"You may not be my husband for long," was her tart reply.

He laughed softly, his warm breath stirring the hair near her face. "Your threat does not convince me, Erica. Your tongue has the boldness of a hawk, but your heart belongs to the dove," he murmured. "With your tongue, you start tempests while your heart seeks the tranquility of the storm's eye. I know you better than you know yourself."

"You can't be sure I'll agree to be your wife," Erica declared with stiff defiance.

"Can't I?" His mouth curved into a cruel smile. "If your sensitive heart did not seek peace at any cost, our marriage would not be a secret today."

She closed her eyes against the frightening truth of his words. When Rafael returned her to Forest at the end of the song, his eyes taunted her with his knowledge. And Erica was still searching for a way to deny it when Forest took her home. She tried to find it in his embrace and failed.

CHAPTER SEVEN

ERICA SNAPPED OPEN her evening bag to make certain she had transferred the house key from her other handbag. The gold key winked reassuringly back at her. She glanced at her petite watch as she stepped into the hallway from her room. Forest would be arriving at any minute.

"Another date with that Granger fellow?" her father's vaguely interested voice asked.

"Yes, the symphony orchestra is giving a concert tonight," she said, smiling.

"I don't think he's going to hear much of it," Vance Wakefield commented, his gaze running admiringly over the gauzy length of lavender-and-blue-flowered chiffon that covered her azure blue evening gown.

"That's the idea, daddy," Erica replied, widening her violet eyes with provocative mischief.

He laughed softly and walked into his study. The corners of her mouth straightened, knowing that as he shut the door, her father also shut out his thoughts of her. Not callously, but simply because there was no reason for him to worry about her.

The doorbell rang and Erica pushed her self-pity aside. She meant to enjoy herself tonight. It might possibly be the last time that she would. Tilting her head at a happy angle, she opened the front door.

"You!" she breathed in astonishment.

Rafael studied her with mocking thoroughness. The black turtleneck beneath his leisure suit emphasized his darkness.

"Yes, Erica, it is I," he replied, thinning his lips into a mirthless smile. "Aren't you going to invite me in?"

Her fingers tightened on the edge of the door, but she didn't step aside to admit him. The paralysis of fear didn't allow any movement.

"What are you doing here?" Her demand came out in an anxious whisper.

"You are going out this evening?"

It was a rhetorical question that required no response, but she gave it anyway. "Yes, I'm going to a concert," she murmured self-consciously, glancing behind him in anticipation of Forest's arrival. "You...you haven't answered my question. What are you doing here?"

His black eyes mocked her persistence, his dark head arrogantly tilted back. "Your week has passed," Rafael stated.

"I have tonight," Erica whispered desperately, bands of fear constricting her throat. Her eyes searched for some sign of compassion in the derisive bronze mask. "Is that why you are here? For my answer?"

"I am here to see your father," he replied with a complacent lift of his brow. "There is something I wish to discuss with him."

"Have you come to tell him a-about us?" Panic removed any pretense of demand from her question.

"Should I?" he parried, the blackness of his gaze burning holes in her despairing hope.

A car door slammed and Erica saw Forest walking swiftly along the stonewalk to the door. Rafael glanced over his shoulder at the approaching man, then brought his gaze back to her face, amusement glittering vibrantly at the dilemma mirrored on Erica's face.

"You won't tell Daddy," she pleaded in a whisper. He stared at her and smiled. "Please, Rafael, don't!"

A strange light flickered in his eyes while his lips twisted in irony. "I will await your decision, Erica," he said harshly.

With Forest only a few steps away, she was forced to open the door and admit both men. Rafael's statement should have reassured her, but it didn't.

Forest greeted him naturally enough, but with curious suspicion in his eyes.

"I'll... let Daddy know you're here, Señor Torres," Erica mumbled, turning awkwardly away from his jeering glance.

Her father evinced no surprise when she announced from his study door that Rafael was here to see him. Deliberately she ignored Rafael's mocking countenance as he walked by her into the study.

"What does he want?" Forest asked grimly, taking her arm.

Erica glanced apprehensively toward the closed study door. "To talk business with Daddy, I guess," she murmured, but she didn't believe that.

There was only one subject that Rafael and Vance Wakefield had in common, and that was herself. Rafael hadn't exactly said that he wouldn't tell him, but the implication had been there that he would keep silent. Yet she didn't trust him.

The evening was ruined before it had even begun. Halfway through the performance, Erica knew that she had to return home. At this very moment, Rafael might be relating the entire sordid tale to her father. The complete absence of color in her face and the tightly drawn lines of strain around her mouth convinced Forest more than her words that she wasn't feeling well. His tenderly solicitous concern made her feel guilty, but not so guilty that she didn't take advantage of it.

With the lingering gentleness of Forest's good-night kiss still on her lips, Erica rapped lightly on the study door and entered. Angry sparks flashed in her eyes when she saw Rafael sitting in a chair opposite her father, casual lordly grace in every line of his form. She had seen his car parked in the driveway, but her expression was one of feigned surprise at seeing Rafael still there.

"Is the concert over already?" Her father frowned as he glanced at the heavy gold watch on his wrist.

"No. Forest received an important phone call that required his immediate attention," Erica lied. "I decided to come home rather than sit through the concert alone."

"A business call at this hour?" Vance questioned.

"You know how that goes, Daddy." She shrugged, trying to read through the pensive, brooding lines of her father's face to discern what he and Rafael had been discussing. "I've become used to it."

"What a pity," Rafael drawled, "to become accustomed to such a thing."

His sardonic expression was openly laughing at her and Erica knew he had guessed why she had returned. He was not at all surprised by her sudden arrival. She sensed that he had anticipated it.

"I've learned to accept it, *señor*," she murmured tautly, putting sarcastic emphasis on the latter word.

There was a satanic lift of a jet-black eyebrow. Then, aloofly, Rafael turned away from her. "It is growing late, Señor Wakefield, and I have taken up too much of your time."

"Not at all, not at all." Her father rose to his feet when Rafael did, waving aside the arrogantly worded apology. "I—" he cast an oblique glance at Erica "—enjoyed our discussion."

"I will see Don Rafael to the door, Daddy," she offered quickly as her father started around his desk.

The absently thoughtful look in his blue eyes frightened her a little. Their discussion had to have concerned her or her father wouldn't be looking at her so strangely.

"Yes, you do that, Erica," he agreed soberly, and wished Rafael a hasty good-night.

Erica didn't trust herself to look at Rafael until the study door was closed behind them. Then she whirled around, the delicately flowered chiffon net billowing about her.

"What did you tell him?" she hissed angrily.

"What do you think I told him?" Rafael countered, his gaze insolently sweeping her face.

"You told him something about us, didn't you?" Erica accused, hating his air of detachment that her anger couldn't touch.

"I said I would await your decision," he reminded her coolly.

"I know what you said," she whispered contemptuously. "I didn't believe you then and I don't now!"

"Do not push me, Erica." The warning was echoed in the clenched line of his lean jaw.

"I want to know what you told him," she repeated. "What devious and evil thing did you say to prejudice him against me?"

His gaze narrowed on her upturned face. "Your father has his own rigid code that he lives by and expects others to live by. I doubt that anyone could influence that code, least of all a stranger."

"Do you honestly expect me to believe that you said nothing about us?" Erica snapped.

Her shoulders were seized in a violent grip. The icy glitter in Rafael's eyes took her breath away as she was vividly reminded of the ruthlessness she associated with him.

"Do you dare to question my integrity when your lips are still warm from another man's kisses?" he demanded harshly, angry forks of lightning darting from the black thunderclouds of his eyes.

"Rafael!" she gasped, helplessly unable to free herself from his iron hold.

She was pulled roughly against his chest, her head snapping back at the abruptness with which she was crushed against him. The muscular hardness of his body drained what little strength she possessed.

"You use my name only when you want something," he growled. "But I will teach you not to be so careless with its use!"

"Y-you're hurting me!" Erica protested weakly, fighting the waves of awareness that flowed in her veins.

"What is it you seek?" His teeth flashed in a jeering smile. "The gentle touch of your lover? Is it his hands that you wish had touched your nakedness first instead of mine?"

His fingers dug even deeper into her soft flesh.

"Rafael!" She moaned in pain, crystal tears shimmering in her eyes.

"You want to be free, no?" His nostrils were distended as he crushed her tighter. "You want to be free of my touch and my name." His silent laughter scorned the futility of such a wish. "But I will not let you go, Erica. You will pay for your foolishness."

Then his mouth claimed hers in a savage possession. Blackness swirled around her. She was incapable of resistance just as she was incapable of responding to his hard, fierce kiss. When he released her mouth, her emotions were as bruised and battered as her swollen lips. His fingers lessened their hold on her shoulders for a second, then let her go altogether. He stepped back, shedding the demon skin for one of arrogant reserve.

"I will pick you up tomorrow afternoon at two o'clock," he told her with an autocratic command. "I will expect your answer then."

"Go to hell!" Erica whispered, pressing the back of her hand to her throbbing mouth.

A cynical smile twisted his mouth. "With you, I am condemned to that."

"Then why make this demand of me?" she protested.

"You are my wife," Rafael said simply, and turned away.

Erica hovered for uncertain moments in the hall-way, her system recovering from the shock of his brutal touch. Then the door to her father's study opened and she spun around to gaze blankly at her father.

"Wh-what did Don Rafael want?" she asked, striving for an air of uninterested curiosity.

A thoughtful look spread across Vance Wake-field's stern face. "He came to see me about some property I own. At least, he said that was why he had come. He asked for my permission to see you, Erica."

"He did?" she breathed. Antagonism surfaced for a brief moment that Rafael should be so certain she would agree to be his wife. "What was your answer?"

"I told him . . . well . . ." He hesitated, wryly shaking his head. "My first instinct was to laugh until I realized he was quite serious. Then I told him that you were seeing Forest Granger, but I told him he had my permission to see you if you were willing."

"He asked me out for tomorrow," Erica told him.

"Did you accept?"

"Yes." She couldn't very well tell him that it had been an ultimatum.

"How serious are you about Granger?" It was the first time in her memory that Vance Wakefield had ever made a direct inquiry. Usually he had someone else do it for him and relay the answer.

"I'm not sure, Daddy," Erica hedged.

"Do you know, I forget sometimes that I'm your father," he commented absently. The statement didn't surprise her, although it wasn't meant to be unkind. "I'm always too busy, aren't I?"

"I understand, Daddy, I'm a big girl now." She smiled wistfully, wishing they were close enough that she could go into his arms and be hugged.

"Forest is a hard, independent and ambitious young man. He isn't intimidated by me, either," Vance Wakefield mused. "His career, his business, is vitally important to him."

"Isn't it to every man?" Erica returned, swallowing the bitterness in her throat.

"No," he sighed heavily. "With some men, the family comes first and will always come first. It's their tradition, their life-style."

A terrible stillness settled over her. "Are you referring to Don Rafael?"

"Not specifically, no," her father replied smoothly. "Although at a guess, I would say that family would have a priority with him."

A priority! Erica thought bitterly. Family and tradition were so important to Rafael that he was determined to keep her as his wife whether she loved him or not. Even he admitted that life would be hell with her, but that didn't deter him.

"Maybe you should think about how much a family means to you before you make any commitment to Forest," Vance Wakefield suggested, running a hand through his thick mane.

Slow anger burned within her. "Did R— Did Don Rafael make that suggestion?" Erica accused.

"Of course not!" His reply was plainly astounded and offended. "Whatever made you think of that?"

She shifted self-consciously under his piercing gaze. "You don't normally talk this way."

"No?" Once again the withdrawn look set in as his mind began to wander. "No, I suppose not. Good night, Erica."

He was already walking into his study and the door
was swinging shut when she added her good-night.
She doubted that he had heard her. That moment of
concern about her future had disappeared as rapidly
and unexpectedly as it had come.

THE HOT October sun blazed down with the heat of
a thousand hells. Erica's teeth grated as she accepted the hand Rafael extended to her as she
stepped out of the air-conditioned coolness of his car.
She had barely said five words to him since he had
picked her up at the house promptly at two o'clock.
The cynically amused tilt of his mouth indicated that
her freezing tactics had not worked. She had shown
no interest in their destination and he had deliberately not enlightened her.

Defiantly tossing back her long hair, Erica glanced
around the downtown section of San Antonio. The
Tower of the Americas loomed benevolently above
them. Its feet were firmly planted in the Hemisfair
Plaza. Perhaps he intended taking her to the top and
throwing her off, thus removing the obstacle of their
marriage.

But it wasn't toward the Tower of the Americas or
Hemisfair Plaza that Rafael led her. Instead he
guided her to one of the many sets of steps leading
from the street level of San Antonio down some
twenty feet to the picturesque walkway along the

river banks. He strolled leisurely by the quaint shops, sidewalk cafés and nightclubs in the commercial area of the riverwalk, indifferent to Erica's displeasure.

The cool serenity of the river, the lush tropical foliage of the gardens, and the age-old trees that shielded the walk from the direct rays of the burning sun soon had their effect on Erica. She had never been able to remain unmoved by the quiet splendor.

Rafael paused to light a thin cheroot, the aromatic blend of burning tobacco strangely fitting the atmosphere. Lean aristocratic fingers hooked themselves in the pocket of his finely tailored trousers as he resumed his leisurely pace.

"It is rare that a man's dreams come true," he commented idly as though voicing his thoughts aloud. For a second Erica thought he was speaking personally and her relaxed expression hardened. "To think that it was once proposed to cover this river with concrete and turn it into a sewer! That visionary architect and the conservationists who fought at his side are to be congratulated."

Erica smiled in silent agreement, wondering if the architect had ever dreamed back in the thirties and the forties that so many people would come to enjoy the graceful beauty of the arched footbridges and the luxuriant crush of greenery. The natural beauty was enhanced, never overpowered by man's touch.

Her glance at Rafael's profile was cool. "I hadn't realized you were familiar with San Antonio and its history."

"You have forgotten, Erica—" he smiled at her absently "—that I am a historian. And I think you have forgotten that most of the Southwest was once ruled first by Spain, then by Mexico."

"Does it bother you to be here in the city that possesses the 'Shrine of Texas Liberty'?" A malicious sparkle gleamed in her eyes.

His regard of her was one of a person overlooking the ineffectual barbs of a child. "You are, of course, referring to the thirteen-day siege by the dictator General Santa Ana of the Alamo."

"And the hundred and eighty-eight men who died there to be free," Erica tossed back.

"Are you asserting your right to freedom?" he inquired lazily. "In the background, do you hear the bugles sounding 'Deguello,' the song of no quarter? It was not only Americans who defended the Alamo to death, but Mexicans, as well. One of your more famous Texas patriots was José Antonio Navarro, who signed the Texas Declaration of Independence. Yet you prefer to look on me as Santa Ana."

"Then don't fight me," she cried angrily. "Let me be free!"

"I am not able to do that." His sardonicism was tinged with resignation. "I, too, must fight for what I believe."

Her hand lifted the heavy weight of her hair and massaged the tense cord in the back of her neck. She had known all along that his stand was adamant, but she had to try.

"Because I will not give in to you," Rafael stated with a note of impatience, "you look on me as ruthlessly cruel, my demands as unfeeling as those dictated by Santa Ana to the peoples of Texas before the rebellion. Look at the unending string of missions founded by the Spaniards throughout your country, Erica. The streak of cruelty is tempered by kindness and devotion. I will be kind to you. You will not be my slave, but my wife. I do not ask for your love in return, but your loyalty to the vows we took. That is the only demand I make of you."

Erica laughed shortly, without humor. "What choice have you given me? Why don't you simply put a gun to my head and shoot me?" Her voice lacked emotion, her hope slowly dying as she resigned herself to fate.

"You are not a lamb, Erica. Do not act like one!" he snapped.

Immediately her temper blazed. "No, I'm not a lamb! All along you've known what my answer would be, the only answer I could give. Now you're going to hear me say it!'' she burst out hotly. ''I will be your wife. Not because I fear you. I am agreeing only because of my father.''

Rafael's face was a study of implacability during her impassioned speech. When she drew a breath to continue, he raised a hand to silence her.

''I am aware that you don't come to me willingly, that I have coerced your agreement. I know you do not love me. There is no need to keep repeating these things. You would do well to direct your energies to convince your father of your interest in me. I am certain you will share my wish not to maintain the pretense of starry-eyed romance any longer than is necessary.'' His clipped statement brought her abruptly back from the satisfying heat of her anger. Color receded sharply from her face.

''Must we do that?'' she murmured, inwardly shivering at the thought of spending endless evenings in his company gazing rapturously at his face, enduring his touch, the incredible warmth his smile could convey. ''Isn't there some other way?''

''So you still wish to run away from that which is unpleasant?'' There was no mockery in his indulgently gentle voice. ''Running only delays that moment when you must face the thing you find so difficult.''

"I have already made the decision," Erica reminded him coldly. "I have agreed to become your wife."

"But you wish to avoid these weeks we must spend in each other's company for the sake of your family and friends. You would prefer to elope with me and stay away until the furor of your actions subsided rather than face the awkward moment when you reject Forest for me."

Erica looked into the placid mask, wondering at his easy perception of her innermost thoughts. As much as she disliked Rafael, she had to admit that she felt the pull of his dark attraction, the lean, muscular body, the strikingly handsome face.

"I'm not a very good liar. I doubt that Forest will believe me if I tell him I'm in love with you and not him," she replied.

"When we are remarried, he will have no choice but to accept it," Rafael stated. "He has asked you to marry him, has he not?"

"How did you know?" Erica frowned, knowing she had never mentioned that.

"Your attorney Jules Blackwell told me, but I would have guessed it anyway. Had Forest suggested an affair instead of marriage, I don't believe you would have made such an instant demand for a divorce." He studied the glowing tip of the thin cigar.

"Forest knows I love him. I told him so." There was a defiant tilt of her head to remind Rafael how unwillingly she was agreeing to his demands.

"People fall out of love." He shrugged dismissively. "Many times the attraction to a member of the opposite sex is mistaken for love. You will need to convince him of that."

Rafael always had an answer, Erica thought dejectedly as she turned away from his unnervingly penetrating regard. At the same moment she counted herself lucky for recognizing that she only found Rafael sexually attractive and had not foolishly believed herself to be in love with him. A heavy sigh vibrated her shoulders. Now she wished she had been blind to the difference, since she was about to commit the rest of her life to him. A pair of rose-colored glasses would be welcome, however inaccurate their view.

"You have my decision. Can't we leave now?" she demanded tightly. "Or do you want to gloat a little longer over your triumph?"

An angry ejaculation was muttered behind her as Rafael spun her around to face him. Lightning currents emanated from the touch of his hands.

"At the moment, I feel no triumph!" he flashed. "If I did not believe that—" As suddenly as he had gripped her shoulders, he released her. "I think you derive satisfaction from igniting my temper." A muscle twitched convulsively in his jaw to indicate that his temper was not fully under control despite the evenness of his voice. "Come, I will take you back to your home."

His brooding silence during the return journey had Erica shifting uncomfortably in her seat. She tried unsuccessfully to block him out of her thoughts, to ignore him as completely as he was ignoring her, but his dark looks and primitive magnetism made that impossible. He was sleek and regally elegant like a jungle cat, and like a jungle cat, there was a strain of savageness that years of civilization hadn't entirely erased.

This man was her husband. She had just committed herself to spending the rest of her life with him—the full enormity of that decision didn't strike her until that moment. A sense of unease crowded around her at the thought of sharing all those intimate moments between a husband and wife with Rafael.

When the car stopped, it took Erica a full second to realize that they were in the private driveway of her home. Her color fluctuated alarmingly as she accepted Rafael's hand out of the car. It troubled her considerably to discover how susceptible she was to his touch. Instead of starting toward the house, he tightened his hand on hers to keep her beside the car. Erica glanced curiously at his slightly narrowed eyes.

"Fate has offered you an easy solution to let Forest know of your change of feelings. He is driving in now—no, don't look around," Rafael commanded as she started to turn in the direction of the approaching car. "All you have to do is kiss me, Erica. He will put his own construction on the rest."

She breathed in sharply, wanting to resist yet knowing that she doubted if she could convince Forest in words that it was Rafael she preferred. Her eyes pleaded with Rafael not to make her do this thing when she was still regretting her decision.

"Decide quickly, Erica," he murmured.

Slowly she moved nearer, drawn more by the seductive sound of his voice than a desire to show Forest her change of heart. The steady rhythm of Rafael's heartbeat was felt by the hands she rested against his chest as she tilted her head to receive his kiss. The gentle insistence of his mouth disarmed her and a pleasant warmth relaxed her tense muscles. A hunger that she had long denied parted her lips so that she was pliant to his touch.

The slam of the car door was unexpected. She sprang guiltily away from Rafael, forgetting completely that the scene had been staged for Forest's benefit. She colored profusely at her shameful lapse, hating that strange power that Rafael held for her physically.

"I couldn't believe it when Lawrence told me you were out with him!" Forest muttered hoarsely. His face was unnaturally pale with controlled rage.

The fierce pain in her heart throttled any words of denial she wanted to say as she gazed hopelessly at him.

"Erica is free to see whom she pleases. There is no understanding between you, is there?" Rafael's arrogantly confident voice inquired.

"I was stupid to believe there was," Forest growled, flicking a maligning glance at Erica. "You've given me your answer, haven't you? I never realized you were so cold-blooded. That must have been what they were talking about when the others called you an ice maiden."

When the last contemptuous sneer had been driven into Erica's midsection, Forest pivoted sharply and stalked back to his car. Her hand raised in a feeble attempt to call him back and explain.

"Forest—" her shaky voice murmured as she took a hesitant step toward his retreating form.

But Rafael reached out and stopped her. "Let him go, Erica," he said firmly. "Don't drag out his agony. Let the killing blow be swift and sure."

A tear glimmered in the corner of her eye, but the fiery light that blazed in the violet blue depths glittered only with resentment.

"You ask that I be merciful," she jeered, "when there isn't any mercy in your heart!"

"I do feel mercy," Rafael stated. "Although I spoke of it for Forest, I meant it for you. I do not want to torture your heart with a love you can never have with this man. Break cleanly from him now so he will not lie between us in the many nights of our lives that are ahead of us."

"How can you speak of such things?" Erica cried, drawing free of his hand in distaste.

"We are married, *mia esposa*. It is not as if we had never known each other in the Biblical way." A lazy smile of complacency curved his mouth. "And I know that Forest has never held you in his arms in the middle of the night, or he would know there is no ice in your veins—huh, *querida?*"

Her cheeks were scorched by the memory his words recalled. She spun angrily on her heel and raced for the house, wondering how many times in the future she would flee from him when she was left with no weapons to attack.

CHAPTER EIGHT

THERE WAS many an eyebrow raised over Erica's sudden break with Forest, and several more when she was seen repeatedly in Rafael's company during the next two weeks.

Their evenings together were always spent attending a concert, theater production or a similar function where there was little need for small talk between them. The distraction of having something to occupy her attention was welcome, although she was never able to completely ignore Rafael. He was much too masculine, and charming when he chose, for any woman to ignore. Yet Erica still refused to like him. How could she when he had blackmailed her into this charade?

All of her friends and acquaintances thought she was extremely lucky to have a man as devastatingly handsome as Rafael paying such marked attention to her. When her replies were less than enthusiastic, they laughed them off as a sign that she wasn't sure she could hold him. Considering the number of her female friends who wandered over during intervals on the pretense of saying hello to her, she tended to marvel at Rafael's seeming indifference to them.

The tinkling of the bell on the shop door announced the arrival of another customer. Donna was in the back room, freshening up after her lunch break. Pushing a welcoming smile on her reluctant mouth, Erica stopped straightening the rack of new dresses to greet the customer. Only it wasn't a customer. It was Rafael.

His dark glance slid past her surprised expression to the back of the boutique, and the wide smile he gave her indicated that Donna must have stepped into view. She was always surprised at the way that smile could take her breath away.

There was only a slight hint of false happiness in her voice when she greeted him. "Rafael—I didn't expect to see you today."

"It is always the unexpected that gives the most pleasure." The caressing tone of his voice reached out to her. "I found myself with the afternoon free and only one person that I wanted to spend it with."

Those black eyes were regarding her with such sincerity that Erica almost believed him until she remembered Donna was listening. The corners of her mouth were tugged downward.

"I hope by that you mean me," she answered in a half-hearted tease.

The intensity of his gaze increased, his brows drawing together in a questioning frown. "Have you not learned that I have eyes for none other but you?" he asked softly. So softly that Erica doubted Donna had heard.

"I think you will have to convince me of that," she whispered, an unknown pain clouding her eyes.

"Erica." The use of her name was an impatient sound that was quickly replaced by his low, cajoling voice. "First I will take you to lunch. You have not eaten, have you?" At the negative shake of her head, Rafael continued, "Then I have something I want to show you."

The last statement astounded her. In all their previous outings, there had been witnesses, crowds of people to insulate her. But Rafael was indicating something entirely different. Erica balked visibly at the prospect of being alone with him.

"Can't it wait for another time?" she blurted. "I really don't have time for more than a lunch break today."

"We're seldom busy on Tuesday." Donna spoke up. "I'm sure I can cope by myself for a few hours, Erica."

Erica pressed her lips tightly together to keep from crying out for Donna to be still. Rafael didn't make it any easier by looking at her with open mockery in his eyes.

"If that is all settled," he murmured complacently, "there can be no more objections, no?"

"No." She shot him a furious look. "I have to get my bag. I'll only be a moment."

A few minutes later they were walking out of the boutique with Donna smiling her goodbye with the enthusiasm of one who has done a good deed. Erica had become accustomed to the possessive touch of Rafael's hand on the back of her waist, but today she took exception to it.

"There isn't anyone watching us," she told him icily, "so there's no need for you to touch me."

"What is it that has made you angry? I do not believe it is my touch." He raised his dark eyebrows.

"I've never stopped being angry," Erica retorted, swinging her head defiantly in his direction. "I've never stopped resenting that you've forced me into this agreement."

They had reached a staircase leading from the river walk to street level. Erica was on the first step when Rafael made her turn around to face him. The one-step advantage brought her eyes level with the ebony blackness of his.

"I wonder which it is that you resent so much. The agreement? Or that I forced your acceptance?" he mused. His hands closed over her hipbones to keep her in place when she would have pulled away.

Her palms were moist and Erica found it difficult to speak clearly. "O-one is th-the same as the other." She was much too conscious of how very near those masculine hard lips were.

"If you say so." He shrugged, laughing silently at her refusal to differentiate. "Why do you hold yourself so rigidly, Erica?"

"I don't see any need to keep up this pretense of devotion in private," she replied quickly.

"How else will you learn to be natural with me?" he mocked.

"I could never react naturally to you," she declared.

An exasperated sigh accompanied the release of his hold. "Let us go and eat before my appetite is completely robbed by your stubbornness."

What little appetite Erica had was gone. Rafael, too, ate very little of his food, as the electrical currents charged the air between them.

"I would prefer to go back to the boutique now," Erica said crisply the minute they were outside the small restaurant.

"This side trip will only take a few minutes of your precious time," was his caustic response.

Often he mocked her, but rarely was he sarcastic. Erica discovered that his acid voice had the power to hurt. There was a sickening knot in the pit of her stomach that she didn't quite understand.

"Where are we going?" she asked hesitantly as he opened the car door for her.

He didn't bother to reply until he was seated behind the wheel and he had maneuvered the car into the traffic. Even then his response was indifferent as though he regretted insisting on this trip.

"A friend of mine bought a house here in San Antonio. It is in need of considerable repair." A sardonic light was in the brief glance he gave her. "Since neither my friend nor his wife is able to be here at this time, he asked if I knew of anyone—any woman who possessed good taste—who would look at the house from a woman's point of view and recommend any changes that might be necessary."

"That's why you're taking me to see it," Erica murmured.

"Why did you think?" Rafael jeered softly. "That perhaps I was luring you off to some isolated place to demand my rights as a husband?"

"I didn't know what you had in mind—" she colored "—but I doubt that you would be so desperate as to take a woman you know would be unwilling."

"That cloak of another man's love that you wrap yourself in will not always protect you, Erica. Do not depend on it too greatly."

To that half-threatening statement, Erica chose not to reply, fearing that she might incite him to prove his point. And she had never had any doubt about his superior strength. She had felt the muscles in his arms and legs and knew they could be steel bands.

The large Mediterranean-style home Rafael parked in front of was bustling with activity. Three gardeners were clearing the months of neglect in the abundant foliage around the front of the house. Towering oaks gracefully arched over the cream yellow façade with its tile roof of chimney red. Other workmen were repairing the loosened mortar of the courtyard walls and replacing broken tiles on the roof.

Rafael led her through the ornate wrought-iron gate into the courtyard with its overgrown walkways and the nearly vine-covered gazebo and from there into the house. Again there were workmen, painters covering the walls with a fresh coat of oyster white and stripping the old varnish from the woodwork. New floors were being laid in other rooms.

In spite of all the commotion, Erica was drawn by the undefinably proud character of the old home. The enormous living room with its high ceilings and mammoth fireplace captured her imagination. She could visualize its elegant grandeur furnished with heavy carved sofas and tables of Spanish design. The breakfast area was surrounded by glass, the individual panes stacked from floor to ceiling.

"Are there any changes, additions that should be made?" Rafael asked her opinion for the first time since the tour had begun.

"I wouldn't change a thing," vowed Erica. In her mind's eye, she was picturing the glassed-in breakfast area abundantly dotted with greenhouse plants to increase the outdoor effect. "Not if you're referring to knocking out walls and altering the basic layout of the rooms," she hastened to add.

"Then you like it?"

"Yes." She looked to him, making no attempt to mask the glow that radiated from her smile. "Your friend is very lucky. This house is a treasure."

"I have told you a small lie, Erica." Rafael turned his enigmatic gaze to the garden beyond the stacked windows. "My friend does not own this house. It belongs to me—to us."

Erica stiffened indignantly. "You tricked me! Why?"

His head was tilted at an arrogant angle so that the impenetrable depths of his black eyes could look down on her. "I believe that if I had told you before we came that it was ours you would have been prejudiced against the house."

She shifted uncomfortably away from his pinning gaze, unwilling to admit there might be any truth to his observation.

"You live in Mexico. Why did you bother to buy this?" she asked with cold scorn.

A savage imprecation was released from his curling lips as he roughly jerked her around to face him.

"I do not know why I allow you to be so insolent," he muttered impatiently. "Yes, Mexico is my home just as Texas is yours. Foolishly I thought it would please you to have a home in San Antonio so that we might spend part of the year here where your family and friends live."

Erica took a deep breath, his thoughtfulness moving her even as she rejected it. He was trying to make her regard him less harshly, lull her into believing that he was really concerned about her happiness. Once she believed that, she would be lost. Rafael's only interest was in himself and getting his own way, and she realized how very expert he was in achieving it. For a moment she had nearly believed that his motive in buying the house had been an unselfish gesture for her.

"I'm sure you will understand that the prospect of sharing any home with you does not fill me with joy," she returned with slow and deliberate sarcasm.

His fingers tightened convulsively on her shoulders and his expression was ominously grim. Erica's heart was beating at a frightening rate as she stared at the taut line of his mouth.

"If you are wise, you will leave without opening your mouth to speak again and wait for me in the car," he ordered harshly, shoving her away from him. "I will have a word with the workmen before I drive you back."

Erica hurried away, knowing her sharp tongue had pushed him too far. She felt sorry for the innocent workman who would bear the brunt of his anger.

That episode, although the house was never mentioned again, brought a decided change in their relationship. They still went out several evenings a week. Any onlooker would have still considered Rafael to be an attentive escort. Only Erica knew how cold and aloof the glitter in his gaze was when he directed it at her, and there was always something very distant in his smile.

Whenever she returned from an evening with Rafael, she was haunted by the specter of those first weeks. Perhaps it was piqued vanity that made her smiles and looks convey an undertone of intimacy as if to draw a similar response from Rafael. But her attempts to flirt with him had only been met by derisive mockery, in itself a sharp reminder that there was nothing between them except a bitter tomorrow with no promise of any sweetness.

The evening before, one of Erica's friends, Mary Ann Silver, had spent nearly the entire interval talking to Rafael about the exhibit he was supervising at the Mexican Cultural Institute. Although a lean hand was possessively resting on the back of her waist, Rafael had not addressed a single remark to Erica.

When Erica's patience had been stretched to the breaking point, Mary Ann had glanced at her with a superior smile.

"Have you seen the exhibit, Erica?" she had inquired.

Rafael's withdrawn smile had been aimed in her general direction as he replied before Erica had a chance. "No, I am taking her on a personally conducted tour tomorrow afternoon."

Erica clamped her mouth tightly shut and smiled wanly, knowing the thought hadn't occurred to him until that moment. Yet at the same time he had managed to convey to Mary Ann that he was eager for Erica to discover more about his avocation.

A gentle breeze stirred the hair along Erica's neck as she and Rafael walked by the Aztec-designed gargoyles that marked the entrance and exit of the Mexican Plaza on the Hemisfair grounds. Exhaling softly, Erica managed to conceal her dispirited sigh. The exhibit could have been interesting, but Rafael's impersonal tour had taken away the fascination. She remembered wistfully his tour of Acapulco that had been so informative and entertaining.

"Where are we going now?" Erica asked as she repressed another sigh.

"Where would you wish to go?" Rafael countered disinterestedly.

"Oh, it doesn't matter," she declared harshly, and increased her pace so that she was carried ahead of him.

If she had hoped he would catch up with her or reach out to slow her down, Erica was to be disappointed. Resolutely she refused to slacken her steps, needing to show him that his indifference was not equal to hers.

In the small square ahead there was a bustle of activity. Pretending a curiosity that she was far from feeling, she headed toward it. The defiant angle of her head indicated that Rafael could follow if he chose.

Then a smile shattered the strained lines around her mouth. Unconsciously she turned it to Rafael as she exclaimed, "Look! They must be going to have an armadillo race!"

As she reached the fringes of the group, she felt his hand on her back and realized he had followed her. But she was much too caught up in the excitement and gay laughter that surrounded her. In the center of the cleared circle was the starting point of the race. The owner-handlers of the armadillos were just entering the circle carrying the strange armor-plated mammals with their tiny ears and thin faces and long bony-plated tails.

"I missed the annual spring race," Erica commented as she glanced back at Rafael. "It's quite an event. There were over twenty-five thousand people there."

The handlers were kneeling down on the center, each holding the tail of his particular armadillo with one hand and cupping the hard breastplate with the other.

"Which one do you think will win?" she laughed gaily, too delighted by the impromptu event to notice the curiously enigmatic light in Rafael's eyes. "I pick the one on the right side. See how he's struggling to get away!"

"I'll pick the quiet one next to yours," Rafael decided in an indulgent tone. "He is wise not to waste his energies so soon."

"He's probably too frightened to move," Erica warned with an impish glance at him. "Mine will beat him easily!"

A half smile of doubt was on his lips when the order was given to release the armadillos. The one Erica had chosen scampered immediately away, only to stop within a few feet, while Rafael's raced directly into the crowd and won.

As Erica half turned to laughingly admit defeat, she found herself jostled against him by the crowd. The sudden contact with his hard and warm length drew a gasp of shock from her. His hands tightened in support, drawing her inches closer. The strange light in his eyes made it difficult for her to breathe.

"I have not heard you laugh so naturally for a long time, Erica," he murmured. Then gently he was setting her apart from him and firmly guiding her toward the car. "What happens to the armadillos now?" he inquired, diverting the conversation back to a less personal subject.

Erica fought off the magnetic pull that wanted to draw her back into his arms. "They make terrible pets, so they're turned loose at the place where they happened to be caught."

Rafael nodded and the aloofness set in again.

A STRANGE restlessness had circled Erica in a cold hand for the past three days, but she couldn't put a finger on exactly what was troubling her. She had sent Donna home and locked up the boutique over an hour ago. There had been no need for her to go home since she had the evening free.

A purpling dusk had begun to settle over the city, adding to her strangely melancholy mood. Her wandering footsteps were drawing her near one of the sidewalk lounges. It was still too early for the night life along the river to begin and the tables were empty. Normally she avoided drinking except at social functions and she especially avoided drinking alone. Yet she found herself sitting down at one of the tables and ordering a glass of wine. She was idly fingering the stem of the untouched glass when a familiar voice sounded behind her.

"My, my, my, if it isn't Miss Wakefield! All alone and without her Latin Romeo," the sarcastic voice declared.

Her stomach tumbled sickeningly as she glanced around. "Forest!" His name came out in an achingly tormented sound.

"I wondered if you would even recognize me." His ruggedly handsome features were drawn with sardonic lines.

Erica had not seen Forest since that Saturday afternoon when he had rejected her, believing that she preferred Rafael to him. Tears pricked her eyes at the harshness that was in his usually warm velvet brown eyes.

"I thought the grand Don Rafael was occupying all of your time now," Forest jeered.

She hunched her shoulders at his stinging arrows. "Don't, please, Forest." She bent her head, her hair swinging down to cover the tear that slipped from her lashes.

He uttered a savage imprecation. In the next instant, she heard swift footsteps carrying him down the few flagstone steps to the river walk proper. Erica sprang to her feet and raced down the steps after him.

The pain hurt too badly for her to let him go this way and selfishly she knew she needed the reassurance that he cared, that somebody cared. Rafael's cold manipulations for the future were simply too heavy a weight to carry alone. Those carefree days with Forest seemed so uncomplicated compared to the twisted path of life she was walking now.

"Forest!" she called out breathlessly.

He hesitated, then turned around sharply. His forehead was creased with an entreating anger. "Erica, there isn't really anything more to say. And I damn sure don't need your pity!"

"I miss you," she whispered, standing in suspended motion before him.

For a second, a hungry light flashed in his eyes before his square jaw was clenched in a rejecting line. "You can't have both of us. You made your choice."

"But it wasn't the one I wanted to make." Her frank protest came out before she could stop it.

He stared at her in silence, then ran his hand through his thick brown hair. "You aren't making any sense," he growled, and started to turn away again.

Her fingers closed over his arm to stop him. "I know I'm not making any sense," she murmured. "I only wish I could explain to you."

The touch of her hand seemed to break the slim control he held. He spun around, taking her by the shoulders and pulling her into his arms. Roughly his mouth caressed her hair as he crushed her even closer to him.

"I must be insane," he murmured. "When I saw you sitting there, I should have walked away."

"I'm so glad you didn't," Erica sighed. The suffocating embrace was easing the cold ache in her heart.

"Why? Erica, why?" He cradled her face in his large hands and tilted it back so she could look into it freely.

Closing her eyes tightly against his beseechingly demanding voice, she shook her head slightly in a negative movement. Her courage failed when it actually came to the moment of explaining her decision.

"If I told you," she said in an aching whisper, "you would only hate me more than you do already."

"I *should* hate you. I actually believed that you loved me as much as I love you. I thought you were seriously considering marrying me. This last month when everyone has so kindly made sure I knew every place you went with that—that—"

The touch of her fingers silenced the sarcastic flow from his mouth. Forest breathed in deeply to regain control.

"I'd almost convinced myself that I didn't care about you any more," he continued with a rueful sigh, "until today. And all the hurt came back."

"I thought it had eased, too." Erica couldn't keep the sadness out of her smile.

The sound of the tourist boat came from the hidden curve of the river and Forest slackened his hold. Reluctantly Erica moved away, wishing they were alone so he could hold her so tightly that she would forget Rafael. Silently Forest held out his hand to her.

"Shall we walk?" he asked quietly.

"I—I don't think we'd better." Erica shook her head.

He looked away grimly. "A minute ago I was holding you in my arms. Now you are saying that you won't even walk with me. For God's sake, are you trying to drive me out of my mind?"

"I don't know what I'm doing," she admitted wryly. Her mind was in a jumbled state of confusion. Her commitment was to Rafael. Seeing Forest again hadn't changed that, nor the circumstances that had prompted her commitment.

"Then explain to me what's going on," Forest said crisply. "Do you find yourself attracted to this—Don Rafael? Is that it? Were you testing to make sure that our love was genuine? That would be ironic, wouldn't it?" He laughed bitterly. "I never even gave you a chance to explain that day. Why didn't you come to me and tell me what a fool I was?"

"Because you weren't a fool," Erica protested.

"What does that mean? You can't be in love with both of us."

"Please, don't ask questions that I can't answer."

"They're simple questions," Forest snapped. "Are you in love with me?"

"Yes, but..." That strange restless confusion returned, leaving her uncertain and apprehensive.

"Are you in love with Don Rafael?"

"No!" Her response came out sharper than she intended and Erica experienced a pang of guilt she couldn't identify. It was silly, because she couldn't possibly care for Rafael.

"Then what is going on?" he demanded. "If you're not in love with the guy, why are you letting everyone, including me, think that you are?"

"I can't tell you." Her voice was choked with frustration.

"Is your father behind this?"

"Whatever made you think that?" she asked in an astonished tone.

"Because this isn't like you at all, Erica. Is he making you see this man to further some business deal he's got in the works?" His voice had become threateningly soft.

Erica's response was immediate and indignant. "Of course not! How could you accuse my father of such a thing? Daddy is insensitive at times, but never to that extent!"

Forest shook his head, trying to shake free of the wall of bewilderment she had erected. "I get this feeling that you're afraid of something. You imply that all this is happening against your will. The only one who's ever been able to make you do anything that you didn't want to is your father, yet you tell me he has nothing to do with it."

"He hasn't." She took a hasty step backward, regretting the impulse that had prompted her to speak to Forest when he would have willingly left her. Rafael had been right. She should have kept the break clean and not let herself become entangled with Forest again.

"Erica, let me help you. I love you," he said earnestly. "I don't begin to understand what's going on, but whatever it is we can face it together."

"You don't know what you're saying." She retreated again. "I think I'd better go."

"Don't you think I would protect you from whatever it is that's frightened you?" Forest demanded.

"I h-have to work it out by myself," Erica refused, knowing how dangerously easy it would be to confide in Forest right now. "I can't involve you."

"I love you," he said quietly. "I am involved."

"Stop—saying that," she breathed. Her palm was raised to ward off the temptation.

"We'll go somewhere else and start over again," he suggested as he saw the slight weakening of her stand. "If—"

"No!"

The second after the strident cry of denial was sounded Erica was running away from him. Her chest heaved with sobs of pain, but fortunately Forest didn't pursue. As much as she tried to shut them out, his last words kept echoing in her mind. Perhaps she had misjudged the depth of his love after all. Maybe he wouldn't desert her if there was a scandalous divorce from Rafael. Her father would be violently angry, but if Forest was there to support her, she might be able to deal with Vance Wakefield.

Then anger and resentment began to build against Rafael. Undoubtedly he had guessed that Forest was the weak link in his plans. He had probably congratulated himself very profusely for getting Forest out of the way so early. Alone, Erica had been vulnerable to his threats and malleable to his proposal. She brushed the tears from her eyes, another impulsive plan taking shape, a plan that could bring her the happiness she had believed was impossible.

In the past her impulsiveness had got her into considerable trouble, including this hated marriage to Rafael. This time she would think it over very carefully, and weigh the risks and advantages before leaping in.

CHAPTER NINE

ERICA PROWLED restlessly about her bedroom, casting impatient glances out the window at the snail-slow movements of the rising sun. The oval clock on her dressing table indicated only half-past six. With an angry movement, she grabbed her bag and bolted from the room.

She had been up half the night making her decision. Even now there were frightened butterflies in her stomach. Rafael had been right when he told her that she had spent nearly all her life trying to run from the things she found unpleasant. He had used that streak of cowardice to his own advantage just as he had done everything else. Only he had cleverly made her believe that remaining married to him and becoming his wife in fact was the way to live up to the obligations and decisions she found distasteful.

His reasoning was about to backfire. Agreeing to his plan had simply been another way of running. She hadn't wanted to face her father's anger or feel his condemnation. She hadn't wanted to take the chance that she would lose Forest's love. Foolishly

Erica had accepted martyrdom, telling herself that she was sacrificing her happiness for those whom she loved. But she had only been taking the path that offered her the least resistance.

Elation swelled like a giant balloon inside her as she imagined the consternation on Rafael's face when she told him that she had seen through his devious plot. She was even beginning to doubt that he would oppose a suit for divorce. After all, his family name was important to him. He would hardly want it dragged through the scandal he had threatened her with if she attempted any legal proceedings.

It frightened her to think how long it might have taken her to discover this if she hadn't seen Forest. Perhaps the whole thing might still blow up in her face. Her father could, at least figuratively, disown her. Forest might not want anything to do with her once he discovered the lie she had been living, but she would be free of the tangled web she had weaved.

The traffic was heavy with people on their way to work. It was seven o'clock before Erica had parked her car and hurried into the hotel where Rafael was staying. The light of certain victory was in her eyes as she started for the elevator doors. Then she changed her mind. She would ring Rafael's suite first and let him wonder why she had come to see him at this hour of the morning. She wanted him to feel the uncomfortable prickles of apprehension before she had the satisfaction of telling him how completely his plan had failed.

She picked up the white house phone, and a wide smile brightened her face as she remembered how childishly frightened she had been the first time she had gone to his room. This time it would be entirely different. She would be the one issuing ultimatums, not Rafael.

On the other end the unanswered ring sounded again and again. Erica nibbled impatiently on her lower lip. She hadn't imagined that Rafael would not be in his room. With a sigh of exasperation, she hung up and dialed the front desk.

"Would you please page Don Rafael de la Torres?" she requested. "I didn't get any response when I dialed his room."

"One moment, please," the courteous voice on the other end replied.

Seconds later she heard his name called over the public address system. Interminable minutes later, the operator came back on the line.

"I'm sorry, he doesn't answer the page."

"Would you try his room again for me?" Erica asked testily.

"What room, please?"

Quickly she gave the operator the number of Rafael's suite. There was a slight pause before the voice responded. "I'm sorry, that suite is not occupied."

Erica frowned. "But I know he's staying here."

There was another request for her to wait and more seconds ticked by slowly. "Señor de la Torres checked out a week ago, miss," the operator told her.

"Checked out? That's impossible!"

"He left a forwarding address here in the city," Erica was informed.

"May I have it, please?" she asked as she rummaged hurriedly through her bag for a paper and pen.

With the address in hand, it wasn't until Erica was back in her car that she realized the address the hotel had given her would take her to the house Rafael had purchased. He had obviously been living there for the past week and she wondered rather curiously why he hadn't mentioned it. Of course, she hadn't evinced the slightest bit of interest in what he did, so she supposed he simply hadn't bothered to tell her.

When she parked her car in front of the house, she was surprised at the transformation that had taken place in such a short time. The riotous foliage was still tropically abundant in front of the house, only now there was a semblance of control. The stone fountain had been scrubbed clean of the grimy moss and ensnarling vines so that water sparkled clearly in its basin.

The scrolled iron gate had a fresh coat of black paint and the thick walls of the courtyard were firmly solid once more. The shaded walkways of the courtyard were no longer losing the battle with the foliage and the view of the freshly painted gazebo wasn't obscured by the previous overgrowth. With an excited quickness to her step, Erica hurried toward the door, eager to see what had been accomplished with the interior of the stately house.

Only when she rang the doorbell did she remember that her reason for coming had nothing to do with the renovation of the house. In fact it didn't concern her at all since she would never be living here. As footsteps approached the door from the other side, she tilted her head to its haughtiest angle.

This forthcoming moment was one she was going to enjoy tremendously. Rafael had been too arrogantly sure of himself. What satisfaction there was going to be in putting him in his place!

A cool smile teased her lips as the door swung open and she was surveyed by a curious pair of dark eyes belonging to an unknown Mexican-American. She guessed that he was a servant of some type, although he wasn't in uniform.

"I would like to see Don Rafael. Is he in?" she asked, making her voice deceptively pleasant.

"Yes, he is in, but—" the man hesitated "—I don't believe he is seeing anyone yet this morning."

"I'm Erica Wakefield. Would you tell Don Rafael that I'd like to see him?"

Her clipped request brought an expressive lift of the man's shoulders that seemed to doubt her name would impress Rafael, but he nodded. "*Sí,* I will tell him."

There was another instant of hesitation when the man debated whether to let her wait outside or invite her into the foyer. He evidently decided that she might be someone of importance and politely asked her to step inside.

While Erica waited in the entryway, she listened to the click of the man's heels on the polished tile floors as he carried her message to Rafael. Her view of the other rooms of the house was limited, but she could see it was now sparsely furnished. The Mediterranean style was the one she would have chosen to match the house's character. She longed for a peep at the breakfast nook, but her curiosity was set aside as she heard the footsteps approaching the entryway.

She stepped forward expectantly as the man reappeared. His dark head inclined graciously toward her, then he smiled with decided apology.

"I am sorry, *señorita*. Don Rafael is unable to see you. He asks that you return in an hour."

Her eyes snapped with amethyst sparks. "The arrogance of that man!" she muttered beneath her breath. She checked her temper, saving it for Rafael. "I will not return in an hour," she said firmly. "You will go back and tell Don Rafael that I want to see him now!"

The man's head tilted to the side as if he was about to refuse, then he decided against it. Again he left her standing in the foyer and disappeared down the cool hallway. His eyes were dancing with secret amusement when he returned a few minutes later. Furiously Erica wondered what Rafael had said.

"Don Rafael will see you now. This way, please," the man invited with only a suggestion of a smile.

The servant walked rapidly back the way he had come and Erica had to hurry her steps to keep up. They passed the living room and the library, and Erica couldn't help blinking in surprise when the man started up the staircase to the second floor.

When Rafael had shown her the house, the staircase was being repaired and she hadn't been able to go through the rooms above. He had said at the time that there were only bedrooms on the second floor. She realized it was early, but she hadn't dreamed that Rafael would not be up. The anger that had built receded rather sharply at this possibility.

As the servant opened one of the doors at the top of the stairs, she found herself nervously clutching the strap of her bag as though it were a weapon. She almost wished she had waited the hour Rafael had suggested, especially when she saw the ornately carved wooden bed that was still unmade. Thank goodness it was empty.

Her heart was thumping unevenly as she stepped farther into the room. The French doors to the balcony were standing open and the aroma of freshly brewed coffee was in the air. It was in the direction of the balcony that the man was leading her.

Rafael glanced up as she hovered between the French doors. "Bring Miss Wakefield a chair and some coffee, Carlos," he instructed calmly.

A large wicker chair was immediately pushed up to the round table where Rafael was seated. Erica was uncomfortably aware of the black dressing robe that Rafael wore, tied at the waist, and revealing the bareness of his legs. As she walked toward the empty chair, she caught the scent of soap and shaving lotion. Her gaze bounced off the glistening wetness of his black hair as she realized that Rafael must have only recently stepped from the shower.

A plate of sweet bread sat in the center of the table and a bowl of fresh chunked pineapple was in front of Rafael. Erica shifted uneasily in the cushions of the winged wicker chair. The man called

Carlos reappeared with a steaming cup of coffee and set it in front of her.

"Would you like something to eat, Erica?" Rafael inquired.

She had difficulty looking into the smoothly bland mask, so she addressed her denial to Carlos. "No, thank you," she refused. Out of the corner of her eyes, she saw the nod of dismissal that Rafael gave Carlos.

At the soft click of the closing bedroom door, she felt the penetrating darkness of Rafael's gaze directed at her. He always succeeded in putting her off balance. Her chin lifted in challenge, determined that it wouldn't happen this time.

"You will forgive me, Erica. I have not yet had my breakfast and I am ravenous." There was little apology in his low voice. "This discussion must be quite serious if it brings you here at this hour of the day. I hope you don't object if we postpone it until after my meal."

She exhaled an angry breath. He seemed not the least bit concerned about what she wanted to discuss, she thought savagely. He was probably quite certain there was no way out for her.

"I don't object," she assured him, thinking silently that he was entitled to his last meal.

Yet it was she who seemed to feel the prickles of apprehension and not Rafael. In an effort toward composure, Erica concentrated on her coffee, trying to ignore the white teeth biting into the juicy pineapple. It was difficult to shake off the sensation of intimacy that sitting across the breakfast table with Rafael created. The gold medallion winked mockingly at her from the vee of his robe.

Finally the pineapple was gone and Rafael seemed disinclined to have more sweet bread. Her teeth were on edge as he refilled her cup, then his, from the coffee server on the table. Leaning back in his chair, he took a slender cigar from the gold case on the table, placed it in his mouth and snapped a flame to it before he glanced at Erica again.

"Would you care to begin?" he murmured.

Erica glared at him, hating the fact that it was he who was so casually relaxed while she sat on the edge of her chair. She folded her trembling hands in her lap.

"I'm not going to go through with your proposal," she replied in a voice that was coldly emphatic.

A dark brow registered amusement instead of surprise. "You're not?"

"No, I am not!" she declared. "I'm going to start the divorce proceedings at once!"

"I see," Rafael replied calmly.

Lazily he rose from the wicker chair and walked over to the balcony railing. Beyond the Spanish lace grillwork was the courtyard, the golden light of the morning sun just beginning to pick its way into the shadows. Erica stared at him in amazement, searching for any sign of anger, any small gesture that would indicate she had thwarted him.

He glanced over his shoulder. "The courtyard is beautiful once again, isn't it?"

Erica pushed herself out of her chair. He was deliberately ignoring her announcement as if it were some child's protest.

"You haven't believed a word I've said," she accused.

Again his gaze swung indolently over her, then returned to the profusion of green below. "Of course I believe you. I don't think you would say what you don't mean." He shrugged, his manner indicating that the matter was unimportant to him. "The gardener has suggested planting climbing roses along the wall. What is your opinion?"

Erica's mouth opened in disbelief. A confused frown crossed her forehead as she walked the few steps to the iron railing.

"I did not come here to discuss gardening, Rafael," she said hotly.

"No?" His bland gaze studied her through the wispy smoke from his cigar. "Is there some uncertainty regarding your decision to file for the divorce?"

"None at all," she avowed, lifting her chin defiantly.

Again there was the expressive lift of his shoulders. "Then what is there to discuss? Why are you here?"

A short, confused laugh came from her throat. She had expected anger, threats, but certainly not indifference, a much more difficult thing to combat.

"I came to tell you I was calling your bluff. Your blackmail isn't going to work. I'm not going to be forced to become your wife," she declared, bewilderedly wondering why she was explaining her reasons.

"That's what you said earlier. But why come here to tell me?"

"I wanted you to know." Her hands raised in confusion.

"Why?" Rafael countered.

"I…" His question baffled her and she groped for an answer. "I suppose I thought it was fair."

There was a complacent lift of his brow. "But according to you, I am a blackmailer as well as your husband. Why should you be fair?"

"I don't know!" Erica murmured angrily. "This isn't making any sense."

"I agree." He smiled lazily. "But I doubt if you have guessed why." He turned slightly to face her. "May I ask what prompted your decision?"

This was firmer ground and Erica tilted her head with defiant arrogance. "I saw Forest last night."

A mocking light entered the dark eyes. "And you discovered you couldn't live without him?"

"No, I discovered that I couldn't live with you!" she retorted sharply. "I don't care how much you threaten me. I don't care if Daddy throws me out of the house. And if Forest finds he doesn't want to risk his career, that doesn't matter, either. I'm simply not going to be your wife any longer!" Her violet eyes narrowed shrewdly. "Besides, I don't think you'll want your precious family name dragged through the mud of a messy divorce."

"I believe, Erica, that you have finally grown up," Rafael murmured.

She looked at him blankly. His calm acceptance was simply too startling to believe. In a daze, she turned toward the courtyard, her fingers closing over the railing as she tried to fathom the reason for his attitude. The smoke of his cigar drifted closer to her.

"Have you spoken to your father and Forest of our marriage?" Rafael was standing beside her, the blackness of his robe visible out of the corner of her eye.

"Not yet," she sighed, then glanced at him sharply. "Why? Do you think you can still talk me out of it?"

He snubbed the cigar out in the gold pottery ashtray that stood beside her. "I can't do that, can I?" he replied with that same casualness that she couldn't understand. "It is a pity, though. Our children would have been beautiful and intelligent, although perhaps too impulsive, no?" He smiled.

His comment brought an unaccountable flush to her cheeks. "And too arrogant," she added.

"*Si*, everyone has faults," he agreed with a mocking grin. "But even in my arrogance I know that I cannot talk you out of your decision. The only way I could persuade you to change your mind was if you loved me. And of course you don't, do you?"

"No," Erica breathed. A tremor raced down her spine, vibrating her nerve ends as she realized how very close Rafael was to her.

"Have you ever wondered what might have happened if you hadn't fled from my yacht that night?" he asked quietly.

"Your yacht?" She turned in surprise.

"You do not still believe it was Helen's?" Rafael chuckled. "It amused me at the time to let you believe that. However, Helen, who happens to be my uncle's wife, was actually staying at your hotel. She had decided against accompanying him to South America on family business. He joined her there a few days after you left. A very happy reunion it was, too."

"But she was an—"

"An American, yes," he supplied. "It isn't uncommon for the Torres family to marry outside their country. My maternal grandmother was French."

"I know very little about you," Erica mused.

"Very little," Rafael nodded, his gaze running lightly over her upturned face. "I know a great deal more about you, yet there are times when you have puzzled me. For instance, I know that you married me to spite your father." The breeze had tossed a lock of her hair across her face and Rafael reached out and tucked it behind her ear, letting his fingers trail down her neck. "Why did you not have me take you back to the hotel when I said that I would?"

Quickly she lowered her gaze from his face, shifting nervously beneath the touch that vividly reminded her of his caresses. She felt shame and embarrassment toward the permissive curiosity that had directed her actions on their wedding night.

"Please, I . . . I don't want to discuss that."

His fingers stopped on her exposed collarbone. "I did not mean to hurt you, Erica." The sincere tenderness in his voice brought an aching throb to her chest.

"You didn't. I mean, you did, but . . ." Embarrassment took over again as she found she couldn't speak of their intimacy with any degree of objectivity.

Gently he lifted her chin. "In the morning, I intended to tell you that you were a very passionate and satisfying lover. I never guessed that you would run from me after we had shared so much."

"Rafael, please!" A weakness descended through her limbs.

"You use my name again." A wry smile curled his mouth, the hard tantalizing mouth that riveted Erica's gaze. "What is it you want of me this time?"

"I don't know," she whispered, her lashes closing on the chaotic thoughts in her mind.

"Do you remember the time in Acapulco when you asked why I didn't kiss you? Where is your boldness now?" he chided.

Desperately Erica reached out for it. "Why aren't you angry? I'm going to divorce you."

"I know." His mouth remained softly gentle and subtly seductive. "How can I feel anger over that? Perhaps if I believed that you were leaving me for another man, I would." Erica gasped sharply, her eyes opening in time to see the half smile. "It is your freedom you want, not Forest."

"What makes you think that?" she demanded in protest.

"Have you not yet learned that it isn't the same when he touches you? The same as it was with us?" Rafael countered. "His caress is pleasant, but not the same."

"I don't know what you mean," she denied vigorously. "The only reason it's different is because I was inexperienced before. I do love Forest."

"A false cloak of love will not protect you."

The vague warning was no sooner spoken than Erica felt the touch of his mouth against hers. Lightly he explored her lips, warming them with the kindled flame of his kiss. Desperately she tried to be analytical in her comparison of his embrace and Forest's, but the strange leaping of her senses made it impossible. His arms curled down her back and gently arched her toward him while her hands encountered the nakedness of his chest.

In a blinding flash, she knew that her responses to Forest had been in answer to his ardency and not aroused by it as was the case with Rafael. Of their own volition, her arms had slipped inside his robe to wrap around his waist. Now she pulled them free and pressed her palms against his chest.

But she didn't have to struggle as Rafael gently let her step back, his hands supporting her trembling frame for a minute before he released her completely. The intensity of his gaze was too disturbing and her pulse was already behaving much too erratically.

"I—I think I'd better leave," Erica whispered after she had taken a deep breath to restore air to her lungs.

"It's a pity you could not love me." His eyes studied the high color in her face. "This thing between us could have been beautiful."

"It would have been the perfect answer for you, wouldn't it?" she agreed dryly. "Now you simply have to find some other woman to bear your children and carry on your precious family name."

His lips thinned. "No other woman will bear my name or my children. You may have your freedom, but I will still be bound by my own chains."

"Aren't you going to contest the divorce?" she frowned.

"The only condition that I make to your freedom is that you tell your father and Forest the truth." The gentleness that had softened his face in the previous moments was replaced by the mask of arrogant aloofness. "Not such a terrible price to pay, since it is one you would have paid if I fought the dissolving of our marriage."

"I don't understand. Why are you giving in?" She shook her head in confusion.

"I never intended to force you to honor our vows," he replied, turning away from her and walking to the table to light another cigar.

"I don't believe you," Erica murmured, watching him warily and wondering what new ploy he was intending to use. "You simply thought you could succeed in bullying me into agreeing. You threatened me with scandal and made me break off with Forest. Why did you go through the deception of taking me out this last month if you didn't intend to marry me in public?"

"Foolishly I thought you might begin to care for me as a person," he said grimly. "I would rather sleep alone for the rest of my life than have a woman who resents my presence in the bed."

He meant every word he said. For the first time Erica knew that Rafael had been deadly serious when he said that he would not marry again. There was a tight knot of guilt in her stomach that she could treat their marriage vows so lightly. She didn't really. She wanted her marriage to be forever, but with a man who loved her, who needed her.

"Rafael, you must marry again," she whispered.

"Do not pity me!" he snapped. "I was aware of the risks I took when I married you. And like you, I will pay the price."

"I wish there was something I could do." Pain snatched at her heart.

"There is," he sighed bitterly. "You can stay my wife."

Erica pivoted sharply away, ruing the damage she had done to both their lives. There was a muffled imprecation from Rafael, then silence. She glanced hesitantly behind her, only to find she was the sole occupant of the balcony. The sound of impatient movements came from the bedroom and she walked slowly through the open French doors. Rafael was viciously yanking a shirt from a wire hanger as she entered. "What are you doing?" The question sprang from her lips unexpectedly.

"I am getting dressed," he replied coldly, pulling a pair of slacks from the closet.

She stood motionless until she saw him unknotting the cord tie of his robe. Then she quickly turned around, his laughter mocking her movement.

"You are still shy, Erica," Rafael commented unkindly.

"I'd better leave," she murmured nervously, and started for the door.

"Wait," he commanded, catching her by the arm before she reached the door. "Give me a moment and I will go with you." There was no request in his ordering tone.

From the corner of her eye, she could see he had his trousers on, but his bronze chest was still bare. "I'm going home," she said curtly.

"I'm going with you."

"Why?" Her demand held accusation for his motives.

His eyes narrowed into black diamonds, hard and cutting. "Because I want to be there when you tell your father about us."

"Don't you think I'll keep my word?" she demanded in a choked voice, hurt by his lack of trust.

His fingers tightened for a fraction of a second before he let her arm go. "I have no doubt you will tell him," he answered tautly. "I realize you believe that I have no mercy, but it is my place to be there to deflect some of his anger."

"Because you're my husband?" Erica taunted, tears stinging her eyes at his unexpected gesture.

"Yes, because I am your husband. Do you think I would make you face it alone?" He turned away from her in disgust.

"Rafael?" she said his name hesitantly.

"What?" he snapped as he roughly put on his shirt, showing a blatant disregard for the expensive material.

"Thank you," she whispered.

He glanced at her over his shoulder, the rigidity leaving his expression. "You are welcome," he nodded, an enigmatic light burning in his eyes.

CHAPTER TEN

AFTER RAFAEL was dressed, he asked Erica's indulgence for a few minutes so that he could make the telephone calls that were necessary to postpone his appointments for that morning. Then he followed in his own car as she drove back to her home.

Parking her car in front of the garage, Erica waited nervously on the flagstone walk for Rafael to join her. As she watched the lean, dark figure approaching her, so composed and controlled, she was suddenly grateful for that underlying steel she had always sensed beneath his strikingly handsome face. Before when it had surfaced, she had fought it as an unruly, frightened horse would fight the commanding hand on the reins.

No one, not even Forest, had ever guessed at her hidden desire to be protected. Independence had been thrust on her and Erica's headstrong willfulness had seized it as a shield to hide her weakness. Yet Rafael knew instinctively that she cringed from her father's displeasure even when she deliberately incurred it. New emotions raced to the front as she

viewed Rafael in this fresh light. He was no longer
threatening her happiness but promising to guard it
in some indefinable way.

Her hand reached out for his physical support,
strength flowing from his grasp of her cold, shaking
fingers. She tried to conceal her dependence on his
presence with a false smile of bravado.

"Shall we go in?" she suggested brightly.

Rafael touched the edge of her mouth where the
tremors of fear were betraying the lack of genuine-
ness in her smile. "Do not be frightened, *querida*."

She wanted to tell him how safe she felt with him
at her side, but the admission wouldn't come out. It
was as if, if she acknowledged the security she felt,
she would have to confess something else.

A firmness straightened the masculine line of his
mouth as Rafael released her hand, letting his arm
curve around the back of her waist. The guidance of
his touch propelled her along the walk to the front of
the house.

A car pulled into the driveway as they neared the
entrance. With a halt of surprise, Erica recognized
the driver as Forest almost instantly. He parked the
car and walked stiffly toward them.

"What are you doing here, Forest?" she asked,
glancing hesitantly at Rafael's unrevealing expression.

"I thought for a minute I was going to be treated to another exhibition," Forest answered grimly, flashing a look of open dislike at Rafael. "I received a telephone call at my office to come here immediately. What's going on, Erica?"

"I..." Her head moved uncertainly toward Rafael.

"I left the message," Rafael stated, ignoring Forest's obvious challenge to explain quietly to Erica. "I believed it would be best if you only had to tell your story once."

She pressed her lips tightly together, moved by his gentle understanding. She had never expected to find security in his embrace, but now she found she wanted to seek it in his arms. Before, the chemistry between them had only been the potent combination of male and female. Only this minute did she realize that his presence offered something more than sexual attraction.

"Thank you," she whispered.

Rafael stared at the brightness of her violet eyes for a long moment, a curious intensity in his dark gaze, then he abruptly swung his attention from her face.

"Shall we go in?" he suggested curtly, the words directed at Forest.

"By all means," Forest jeered.

Suddenly, in Erica's eyes, Forest turned into a stranger, someone she barely knew at all, and she found herself edging closer to Rafael. It was difficult to remember that she had despised him and his trickery only a few hours ago.

Lawrence was in the hallway outside her father's study as the trio entered the house. There was undisguised speculation in the look he darted at the three of them, but his voice was professionally calm when he spoke.

"Mr. Wakefield is expecting you if you would like to go right in," he said, motioning in the direction of the closed study door.

Rafael had evidently contacted her father at the same time as Forest, Erica decided, experiencing a sense of relief that they weren't barging in totally unexpected. The reassuring pressure of the hand on her back was removed as Rafael stepped forward to open the door. It wasn't replaced as he allowed Erica and Forest to precede him into the room. Vance Wakefield seemed to be in an amicable mood as he rose from his desk to greet the two men and his daughter.

The smile on his face didn't cover the sharpness in his blue eyes when he turned to her. "I see I've evidently been chosen as a mediator in this lovers' triangle."

Erica was perched on the edge of a leather chair. Her gaze skittered across the room to where Rafael was relaxing in the large leather armchair and on to Forest who was sitting nearest her in a watchful silence.

"You're not exactly a mediator, Daddy," she responded quietly, twisting her fingers together on her lap. She breathed in deeply, searching her mind for a place to begin. "I don't know of any way to start without sounding melodramatic." She smiled weakly at the ice-blue regard. Her gaze darted immediately to Rafael and clung to the vague reassurance she saw in his eyes. "You see, Daddy, Rafael and I are married."

"*Married?*" The expected explosion came from Forest instead of her father. "Do you mean you had me come over here just to learn that you'd married him? You cold-blooded little female!" he shouted as he pushed himself out of the chair.

"Sit down, Señor Granger," came Rafael's clipped order. "You will hear my wife out before you leap to condemn!"

Forest glowered at him, then sat back in his chair. Erica turned away from the disgust in Forest's expression, her heart leaping at Rafael's quick defense.

"This was a bit sudden, wasn't it, Erica?" her father said quietly with an underlying hint of disapproval. "Not that I have any objections to Don Rafael."

"Actually—" she stared at her tightly clenched fingers "—I met him almost two years ago when we were in Acapulco. I didn't know who he was at the time—that is, I thought I knew." The red of embarrassment stained her cheeks as she raised her head. "I believed he was a fortune hunter. I married him the night you flew to Houston, Daddy."

An uncompromising coldness entered her father's face. "Are you saying that you've been married to him for nearly two years?" he demanded.

She nodded, squarely meeting the anger building in his eyes. "I did it to spite you. I know it sounds childishly stupid now, but then I only wanted to make you sorry for ignoring me when it was supposed to be our vacation. When I found out you'd left, I was too frightened to tell you what I had done."

Vance Wakefield made no comment. He simply looked at her with icy displeasure as if saying that he wasn't surprised that she had behaved so foolishly. She was a willful female without an ounce of sense.

"I suppose he's been blackmailing you all this time," Forest muttered, glancing at Vance Wakefield. "We only have his word that he is who he says he is."

There was a thread of finely honed steel in Rafael's voice as he responded to Forest's implication. "Señor Wakefield has already made discreet inquiries of the local Mexican Consul to verify my identity."

"That's true. I did," her father replied without any apology.

"And he's why you didn't accept my proposal, isn't he?" Forest said grimly.

"I couldn't very well agree to marry you when I was already married to Rafael." Erica laughed bitterly.

"At least you were sensible about that," her father murmured dryly. "I suppose I should be grateful that you didn't get yourself into a bigger mess."

"Your criticism of Erica is unwarranted," Rafael inserted smoothly as Erica flinched at her father's cutting remark. "Everyone is capable of mistakes."

"My daughter has a penchant for trouble," Vance Wakefield bristled, "and then expects me to get her out of it. I don't think I would be wrong if I said that she's made this confession today in order for me to arrange an annulment so that she'll be free to marry Forest."

"An annulment isn't possible." A stunned silence followed Rafael's softly spoken voice, and Erica flushed under Forest's accusing glare. "It is true that

Erica ran away after we were married, but not until the morning after our wedding."

Forest cursed beneath his breath, while her father's eyes narrowed into ice chips of polar blue. Erica's couldn't bear their joint censure and bounded to her feet, turning her back to them and hugging her arms about her churning stomach.

"If your intention was to divorce him, why have you been seeing him constantly this past month?" Forest demanded.

Erica glanced over her shoulder at Rafael, strangely unwilling to tell of the way he had forced her to see him. He returned her look steadily and answered the question for her.

"Because my wife believed that I would not grant her a divorce. I told her if she did not break off with you and begin seeing me, I would go to her father and tell him of our marriage, knowing how highly she valued his opinion of her. Erica came to me this morning and told me she was going to tell her father the whole truth and face the consequences."

"I would like to know why you married my daughter and kept silent about it." Her father's sharp gaze swung from Erica to Rafael.

But Rafael was immune to his disapproval as he studied Erica's face before replying. "I married your daughter because I loved her, and for no other reason."

"That's not true," Erica gasped. "You only married me so you could have children!"

"You never asked why I married you," Rafael reminded her cynically. "You have never considered what my reasons might have been. Yes, I want children, but there were any number of women who would have married me and given me children. I guessed that you didn't love me the night I married you, or at least, not as fully as I loved you. But in my arrogance—" he smiled in self-mockery "—I believed you would come to return my love in time. I never expected to find you gone in the morning."

Erica stared at him in wordless amazement, the knowledge that he loved her jolting through her like an electric current.

"As you once pointed out, *querida*," Rafael continued, "I have a vast quantity of pride. When I found you in San Antonio, you demanded a divorce and claimed to be in love with another man. I could hardly fall to my knees and declare my love for you under those circumstances."

"If you knew she loved me," Forest inserted, "why didn't you do the decent thing and set her free?"

Rafael's aloof gaze swung arrogantly to Forest. "Because I knew you could never make her happy. Oh, perhaps for a little while." His hand moved in a short dismissive gesture. "But you are too much like her father. A few months after your marriage, you would begin taking her for granted, pushing her aside to further your career. You might have one or two children to occupy her time, but the love for a child can never take the place of the love that a man and woman share. I had hoped that Erica might begin to care for me in this past month, but she has not. So I have agreed to her request for a divorce and will not contest it."

He rose lightly to his feet and turned to her father. "Do not be harsh with Erica. The sensitivity you see as a weakness, I see as strength. She accepts your affection and returns it tenfold. Not many parents can say that of their children." His glance encompassed Erica and Forest. "There is no more of the story that needs to be told. My presence is no longer required. *Buenos dias.*"

Silently, almost in a daze, Erica watched him walk past her to the door, with no more than a gracious nod in her direction. When the door closed behind him, she knew that she would never see him again. There was no elation, no sense of relief, no feeling of victory that she had finally achieved her freedom, in word if not yet in deed. There was only a frightening emptiness, a void as if some precious part of her had walked out the door, as well.

"I'll call Jules," her father said gruffly. "He can start drawing up the papers for the divorce."

"No!" The denial was spontaneous and firm. "No, there will be no divorce," Erica declared.

"Don't be idiotic!" Forest cried angrily. "The man is giving you your freedom. We can be married."

"I don't want to marry you." She looked into the strong square-jawed face, seeing beyond the rugged exterior for the first time. "I don't love you, Forest. I'm sorry, but you're just a shadow of my father. You're so very like him that I'm surprised I didn't see it before. I love my father, but I don't want to be married to him."

"You certainly don't think you're in love with Rafael, do you?" Forest laughed shortly in scornful disbelief.

Erica said nothing **for** a second before she replied slowly and with increasing sureness. "Yes, yes, I think I am."

"Don't make another mistake, Erica," her father cautioned, but there was nothing dictatorial in his voice.

But Erica was already racing out of the house and around to the side where Rafael had parked his car. The door was open and he was about to step in when he saw her. She stopped, then hesitantly walked toward him, trying to fathom the aloof mask for some sign that she wasn't too late. The words that would be said between them in these next few moments would determine the outcome of her future.

"Rafael." His name came from her parched mouth in a croaking whisper and she wished for the courage of the matador when he faced the black bull in the ring.

"Yes. There is something more you require?" Impatience edged his low voice.

Erica moistened her lips nervously. "I don't want a divorce, Rafael."

If anything, his expression hardened. "I do not need your pity. Leave me to see what peace I can find."

"I don't pity you, Rafael," she insisted. "I pity myself for perhaps finding out too late that I really love you. I know there's nothing I can say to make you believe me, but it's true all the same. I do love you."

"You are only grateful," he corrected harshly, "grateful that I shouldered some of the blame for our stupidity and blunted your father's anger. Do not hide your gratitude in words of love."

"I don't know when I began to love you. I only know I realized it a few moments ago when you walked out of the study and part of me went with you." Erica refused to give up. "It was as if a fog lifted and I understood why you had this strange power over me every time you touched me. Don't you see, Rafael? I could never let myself love you before because I thought you'd married me for my money. I pretended that I let you make love to me because you were so physically attractive. Then I was terrified that I was promiscuous. Only I found out that no other man made me feel the way you do, not even Forest. When you came here and I discovered you weren't a fortune hunter, you backed me into a corner and demanded that the marriage become a reality. But I believed you wanted it to save your family from the shame of a divorce and so you could have children, not because you cared for me."

His attitude remained unreachable and she clapped a hand to her mouth as a bitter laugh of discovery ripped her throat. Tears scalded her eyes and trickled from her lashes down her cheeks as she turned swiftly away from him.

"What a fool I am!" she exclaimed. "That was all just a ruse in there with my father, wasn't it? You only said you loved me to save my pride. You never expected me to take you seriously, but I don't care!" she declared wildly. "You wanted a wife and children. Well, I'm your wife and I will give you children. But I love—"

"Stop it!" Savagely Rafael grabbed her by the shoulders and spun her around. The iron control was gone and an inverted anger was in its place. Despite the vicious shake he gave her, the tears didn't stop as she gazed at him with the full futility of her love in her eyes. "You are giving in to an impulse. You do not know what you are saying," he snapped.

"And you're too arrogant to believe me!" she cried.

In the next instant, the arms that had so rigidly held her away crushed her against the hardness of his chest, locking her in an embrace that was exquisite punishment. Hungrily his mouth probed hers until she throbbed with a feverish ache for him. Even when he later untwined her arms from around his neck, she was blissfully aware of his reluctance.

"I do love you, Erica, *mia esposa*," Rafael declared huskily, and the burning fire in his gaze convinced her beyond all doubt.

"Why did you wait so long to come for me?" she whispered, touching the face that she now had a right to caress.

"So long?" He laughed softly. "Ah, my love, when I found you were not on board the yacht, then later discovered you had checked out of the hotel, I flew to San Antonio immediately. No one could or would tell me where you were. I waited here for nearly two weeks before I received word that my father had suffered a stroke. I had to return to Mexico. Circumstances have kept me there all this time."

"And your father?" Erica prompted.

Pain flickered for a moment in his eyes. "He died this last spring."

"Oh, darling, I'm sorry." Her lips trembled in sympathy. "I wish I'd been there with you."

"You did not love me then." Rafael kissed her mouth lightly so she would know he meant to inflict no pain with those words.

"You do believe that I love you," Erica sighed, resting her head contentedly against his shoulder as his arms tightened around her.

"You must tell me that tomorrow and every tomorrow after that." The husky command was muffled by the soft skin of her throat.

"I promise I will," she whispered as she felt the melting of her bones beneath his fiery caress.

"Every morning that I woke without you in my arms made the night we shared so bittersweet," Rafael murmured. "Several times I have thought you were about to discover you loved me. Then I gave up hope. When you were with me, you seemed to become more unhappy and I knew I must set you free."

"I don't deserve you. You were right when you said I was selfish." She gazed sadly into his face.

"I hope you cannot bear to let me out of your sight," he vowed. "It has been sweet torment to be so near you and not touch you or show you the way I cared. If you had learned Spanish before, you would have known how much I loved you on our wedding night aboard the yacht."

"Where is the yacht?" asked Erica, now cherishing the memories of that night.

"In Acapulco, waiting for you to return," he answered.

"Mañana," she murmured the name of the yacht. "Let's go there."

"We will spend our honeymoon on board after we fly to my home tomorrow so my family can meet you," he declared.

"Do they know about me?"

"Yes," Rafael smiled tenderly. "Not that you are my wife, but I have spoken of you and of my intentions to make you my wife. My pride would not let them think ill of you nor pity me that I had lost you. We will have another small wedding at the church in the village near my home. You do not mind?"

"No, I'd like to say our vows again. But, Rafael—" a shy pink heightened her face as the desire to feel his touch swept over her "—must we wait?"

He drew in his breath sharply. "You are my wife." From his pocket, he removed the signet ring and slipped it on her finger. "Your friend Jules Blackwell returned it to me. I told him I loved you and would not leave until this was on your finger again."

Ring in the New Year with babies, families and romance!

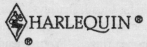

NEW YORK BLOCKBUSTER SWEEPSTAKES
OFFICIAL RULES—NO PURCHASE NECESSARY

To enter, complete an Official Entry Form or 3" x 5" card by hand printing the words "New York Blockbuster Sweepstakes" and your name and address thereon and mailing it in the U.S. to: New York Blockbuster Sweepstakes, P.O. Box 9076, Buffalo, NY 14269-9076, or in Canada to: New York Blockbuster Sweepstakes, P.O. Box 637, Fort Erie, Ontario L2A 5X3. Limit: One entry per outer mailing envelope. Entries must be received no later than 1/31/97. No liability is assumed for lost, late, damaged, nondelivered or misdirected mail. Entries are void if they are in whole or in part illegible, incomplete or damaged.

One winner will be selected in a random drawing to be conducted no later than 2/28/97 from among all eligible entries received. Prize consists of a 3 day/2 night weekend for two (Friday-Sunday) including round-trip air transportation from commercial airport nearest winner's home, two nights hotel accommodations (one room double occupancy), at the New York Marriott Marquis Hotel, and a pair of theater tickets to a major Broadway show (approx. prize value: $2,400 U.S.). Travelers must provide their own transportation to and from the commercial airport nearest winner's home; are responsible for taxes, tips and incidentals; must execute and return a Release of Liability prior to travel; and must depart and return prior to 12/31/97.

Sweepstakes offer is open only to residents of the U.S. (except Puerto Rico) and Canada who are 18 years of age or older, except employees and immediate family members of Harlequin Enterprises, Limited, their affiliates, subsidiaries, and all agencies, entities and persons connected with the use, marketing or conduct of this sweepstakes. All federal, state, provincial, municipal and local laws apply. Offer void wherever prohibited by law. Taxes and/or duties are the sole responsibility of the winner. Any litigation within the province of Quebec respecting the conduct and awarding of prize may be submitted to the Régie des alcools des courses et des jeux. Prize is guaranteed to be awarded; winner will be notified by mail. No substitution for prize is permitted. Odds of winning are dependent on the number of eligible entries received.

Potential winner must sign and return an Affidavit of Eligibility within 30 days of notification. In the event of non-compliance within this time period, prize may be awarded to an alternate winner. If prize or prize notification is returned as undelivered, prize may be awarded to an alternate winner. By acceptance of his/her prize, winner consents to use of his/her name, photograph or likeness for the purpose of advertising, trade and promotion on behalf of Harlequin Enterprises, Limited, without further compensation unless prohibited by law. In order to win a prize, a resident of Canada will be required to correctly answer a time-limited arithmetical skill-testing question by mail.

For the name of the winner (available after 3/31/97), send a separate stamped, self-addressed envelope to: New York Blockbuster Sweepstakes 4815 Winner, P.O. Box 4200, Blair, NE 68009-4200 U.S.A.

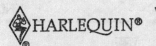 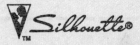

Win an exciting weekend for two in New York City at the

NEW YORK

Marriott.

MARQUIS

including return airfare and tickets to a Broadway Show!

You and a guest could be on your way to the Big Apple, courtesy Harlequin Enterprises and the New York Marriott Marquis! See Official Sweepstakes Rules for more details.

NEW YORK BLOCKBUSTER SWEEPSTAKES
OFFICIAL ENTRY FORM

To enter, complete an Official Entry Form or a 3" x 5" card by hand printing "New York Blockbuster Sweepstakes," your name and address, and mail to: in the U.S.: New York Blockbuster Sweepstakes, P.O. Box 9076, Buffalo, NY 14269-9076, or in Canada: New York Blockbuster Sweepstakes, P.O. Box 637, Fort Erie, Ontario, L2A 5X3. Limit one entry per outer mailing envelope. Entries must be received no later than 1/31/97. No liability is assumed for lost, late, damaged, nondelivered or misdirected mail.

NEW YORK BLOCKBUSTER SWEEPSTAKES
OFFICIAL ENTRY FORM

Name: _____

Address: _____

City: _____

State/Province: _____

Zip/Postal Code: _____

KNL

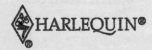 

Not The Same Old Story!

Exciting, emotionally intense romance stories that take readers around the world.

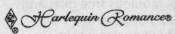

Vibrant stories of captivating women and irresistible men experiencing the magic of falling in love!

Bold and adventurous— Temptation is strong women, bad boys, great sex!

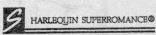

Provocative, passionate, contemporary stories that celebrate life and love.

Romantic adventure where anything is possible and where dreams come true.

Heart-stopping, suspenseful adventures that combine the best of romance and mystery.

 Entertaining and fun, humorous and romantic—stories that capture the lighter side of love.

Look us up on-line at: http://www.romance.net   HGENERIC

You're About to Become a *Privileged Woman*

Reap the rewards of fabulous free gifts and benefits with proofs-of-purchase from Harlequin and Silhouette books

Pages & Privileges™

It's our way of thanking you for buying our books at your favorite retail stores.

Pages & Privileges™

✂

```
┌─────────────────────────────┐
│  [book]  PROOF OF     │
│          PURCHASE     │ NYT-PP20
│  Offer expires March 31,1997  │
└─────────────────────────────┘
```

**Harlequin and Silhouette—
the most privileged readers in the world!**

For more information about Harlequin and Silhouette's PAGES & PRIVILEGES program call the Pages & Privileges Benefits Desk: 1-503-794-2499

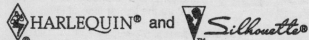

HARLEQUIN® and Silhouette®

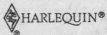

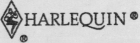